SS & M

Being Excerpts from the Nazi Death-Head Files

by

WILLIAM MALTESE

The Borgo Press
An Imprint of Wildside Press

MMVII

CONTENTS

Chapter One..5
Chapter Two..31
Chapter Three..47
Chapter Four..65
Chapter Five..83
Chapter Six..107
Chapter Seven 121
Chapter Eight...135
Chapter Nine..147

For Jardonn…

…Who persuaded me to bring this up
and out of its deep and dusty storage trunk

CHAPTER ONE

"YOU ARE NOTHING MORE THAN a piece of meat," Colonel Saber said, pacing in front of what was once a pretty young woman. "Actually, you are less even than meat. Meat can at least be eaten; not even a Jew would eat fellow pig, would he?"

His words barely penetrated to Marta's brain. There'd been so much pain, so very much, that the shrieking hum of it still remained to the distraction of everything else. It played loudly against her one punctured eardrum. It pulsed throughout her body like a second heartbeat.

Colonel Saber moved Marta's head with the tip of his highly polished black boot. In a way, it was a shame that she'd been so difficult. She had, after all, been a very attractive member of her subhuman species. She could have had a few more months left to live in one of the special prostitution establishments staffed by non-Aryans. And, not even Saber had anything against a German fucking a Jew. That was certainly no different than fucking a dog: something done by at least one member of Hitler's High Command.

Marta had, though, been difficult. She'd been next to impossible. Saber was always surprised to find how hard these *things* fought to preserve the members of their species. They really were quite impossible. There was no way you could convince them of their inferiority, even if you lined up all the scientific facts by way of proof. They were all brainless, driven to procreate and persevere, like baboons at rut in the trees.

Marta's mouth ran blood. Some of the blood was crusted. One of the first things Saber had done when Marta had entered the room was strike her across the face with the ivory and gold handle of his swagger stick. He'd broken her front teeth. She'd spit the pieces up on the floor. They were still there, fractions of white in a pool of coagulated pink saliva.

The bitch had looked so surprised when he'd hit her. They *always* looked surprised. What did any of them expect when they got hauled here? Did they think they were being asked for schnapps? Hell, no! They couldn't possibly think that. Too much of what did go on behind these closed doors, in these cellar cubicles, in these interrogation rooms, had already leaked out. Yet, one after the other, people walked in, just like Marta, arrogant as ever, thinking that what had happened to the others would certainly *not* happen to them. Unfortunately for them, they were wrong in their collective assumption.

"Oh, Marta Solomon, alias Marta Steiger," Colonel Saber said, shaking his head in disbelief, "how can you persist in not telling us what we want to know? In the end, you shall tell us anyway. Then, what? All that you've gone through, and all that you *will* go through, will have been for nothing. For absolutely nothing. And what will you have gained? Even if you'd lived to look in a mirror, you'd only wish yourself dead. So, why not just tell us what we want to know?"

* * * * * * *

WHAT SABER AND HIS SUPERIORS wanted to know were the names. Jewish names. Names of certain people existing within the very Third Reich who had gotten their present positions by subterfuge.

Smelling their extermination, like buzzards sensing decaying carrion on the wind, many Jews had fled. Others had, for one reason or another, stayed behind. Most of those who stayed had been rounded up. Some, though, had been clever. They'd changed names, forged papers, bribed petty bureaucrats. They now masqueraded as pure Germans. Such utter audacity!

And here was little Marta Solomon who would soon be naming names, just like little Mehetabel Moiyan had told Saber of the Steiger family—who hadn't really been Steigers at all.

"Come now, Marta," Saber said. "I shall give you one more chance. You tell me what I want to know, and I'll call my men to take you out of here. Wouldn't you much prefer a nice clean bed to this cold and hard floor?"

Oh, God, she hurt! Mentally, Marta tried to isolate one single place inside or out which *didn't* ache. She was unsuccessful. She hurt *everywhere*. She was just one big agony. And this German bastard was insinuating there would be more pain, more agony, more hurt, unless…

God help her. She couldn't tell him. She couldn't! She'd been Melissa's friend forever. If she talked, they would bring Melissa here. They'd bring Anna and Wilhelm. How could Marta talk and subject any of them to this?

Saber motioned for the two soldiers who stood by one wall. They came at his nod. They undoubtedly thought Saber was going to give them leave to again use the girl's body for their cocks. Josef had especially enjoyed Marta's tight virgin ass. Karl was less excited than he might have been, because he liked mouth; Saber had ruined that for Karl with the first blow of the swagger stick. Still, Karl had fucked the girl in the cunt once and, then, taken sloppy seconds up her ass. His cock was hard again. It was a big cock, evident in its present ridging of the young soldier's left pants leg.

"I want her moved over there," Saber instructed, pointing to a spot across the room. He was afraid he was going to have to disappoint them. After all, he had given them first whack at the little bitch. That was better treatment than they'd have gotten from any other interrogator. Take Stillman, for instance. Stillman personally went through mouth, cunt, and ass, in that order. And when he finished with each, he made sure no other cock would follow suit. The women and girls who came out of his sessions were hardly recognizable even as members of a subspecies. Stillman's assistants invariably came out with their hard cocks still large, their balls turned blue from frustration.

If Saber believed in sharing (after all, the way things went, you never knew when one of the soldiers here today would be promoted and useful tomorrow), that didn't mean, he was generous to the exclusion of his own passions.

Saber's cock was hard. It had been hard for a long time. It had gotten harder when Saber had seen Josef fucking the girl's ass, harder yet when he'd seen Karl fucking her cunt and then her butt hole. Then, if possible, it had gotten even harder as Saber had been forced to proceed to more violent methods of interrogation when the girl refused to talk.

Marta groaned when they hefted her. They treated her with less concern than they would a sack of potatoes. But, why should she expect any more at this late date?

They dropped her, back against the floor, after having half carried and half dragged her to where Saber had indicated. They looked disgustedly at the mess her bleeding had left on their hands and clothes. There was something especially disgusting about a Jew's blood. It never seemed to wash out, and it stunk like pig sty.

"Drop the bar, Josef," Saber instructed. There was a foot-long bar hung by its center from a rope suspended from the ceiling. From each end of the bar was suspended a length of chain. By untying an end of the rope from a bracket trailing one wall, the weight of the bar and its chains lowered, via a dual pulley system.

"My little Jewess pig bitch," Saber said and nudged Marta's body with his boot toe to be sure she was still conscious. "Do you know what butchers do with their meat? They hang it on meat hooks. They hang it for days and days and days.

Marta stirred. She tried to sit up. Her head throbbed. Her vision kept going in and out of focus. Colonel Saber's voice came to her on waves: loud, soft, loud, nonexistent. What was he saying? Meat? Hanging? What did he want? What did any of them want? Why couldn't they let her alone? She was so tired. She hurt so much.

Saber went to the cabinet by one wall. He knelt. He opened the third drawer on the left. He lifted out two large hooks, shutting the drawer before standing.

"Aren't these beautiful?" Saber asked, extending one hook in each hand. They were made of polished steel, each curved wickedly to a barbed point. They were about a foot across at the curve. At the opposite end from the point, each hook had a dime-sized eyelet. "Made especially for hanging sow."

They'd smashed her face. They'd raped her cunt and her ass. They'd beat her. They'd cut her. What would they do to her now? Hang her like a pig? On hooks? *Oh, God. Oh, God. Oh, God!*

Saber watched for Marta's reaction. It was very difficult to read what the girl was thinking. Her face was such a distorted mass of twisted flesh. Her eyes were puffed and almost swollen shut. Her nose was obviously broken, nostrils clotted with blood, set off-center. Her mouth was twisted almost into a grin, lips cracked and bleeding.

Josef had lowered the bar and its chains to Saber's chest level. The Colonel reached for one of the chains. He snapped the end of the chain to the eyelet of one hook. He repeated the process with the other chain, the other hook.

"Prop her up, Karl," Saber said.

Standing at the girl's head, Karl squatted and slipped his hands underneath her armpits; he tugged her body upward and shuffle-walked forward.

Marta found herself in a partial sitting position. Her back was propped against Karl's knees. The German soldier held her, secure.

Saber stepped to straddle Marta's body, facing toward Karl. Saber squatted, the ass of his trousers hovering above the cum and blood-drenched hair on the girl's pussy. He nodded toward Josef by the wall. Josef lowered the bar, chains and hooks farther. Saber caught the hooks in his hands. He held them for Marta to see.

"You might as well tell us what we want to know," he said and moved the metal hooks so that the light from the bare bulbs reflected in the polished steel. "We'll soon have both your parents and your sister. If you don't talk, they will."

That told Marta one thing. So far, her parents and sister were still safe. Had they come back to the apartment and seen the cars? Had they seen her being dragged away? Had they fled? To freedom? Where was there freedom? Hitler's men were everywhere. There were so few havens for the Jews anymore; none of them close at hand. This enemy Colonel was probably right. They probably would capture her parents. They probably would capture her sister. Marta shuddered, not at her own pain and anguish, but at what would soon become of those she loved.

"Names, please," Saber said. When Marta didn't answer, he sat his ass even nearer her cunt. He dropped both of his knees to the floor, holding her lower body encased between his bent legs. He nodded for Karl to hold the girl's arms.

Karl caught first one of Marta's arms and then the other, pulling them straight back behind her body. He put a knee in the small of her back. The girl's ribcage thrust forward.

With his left hand, Saber reached out to palm Marta's right tit. The flesh was warm, full-blown. With his right hand he brought the sharp end of one hook over and into place. The point touched the pink flesh on the underbelly of Marta's right breast.

"Names?" Saber asked again. When Marta didn't answer, Saber stuck her tit with the barbed point. With persistent pressure, he drove the point inward and upward, feeding more of the curved metal into yielding flesh.

Marta thought there could be no greater pain than that she'd already endured. She was wrong. The searing jolt of agony now sun-bursting from her right tit to the rest of her body was unbearable in its extreme. All her eyes registered were staccato flashes of bright red. She threw her head back, her throat taut with stretched tendons. She opened her mouth to scream, but she couldn't seem able to make any sounds. Her lips moved; her tongue lolled.

Saber kept force-feeding the hook into the tit until the barbed point of the hook blossomed with a spouting of blood through the top of the creamy breast. Blood oozed outward from the emerging point, drooling over the upper curvature of pale flesh. Beneath his butt, Saber could feel the woman's body jerking like a fish out of water. He adjusted the lay of his cock against his left leg. His cock was hard, very hard.

Saber recognized the symptoms of upcoming unconsciousness in a victim: the glazed eyes, the drooling mouth, and the slack facial features. He retrieved an ampoule from the pocket of his uniform and cracked it beneath Marta's nose.

The pain-numbed girl inhaled the released fumes. She took the foul smell deeply into her lungs and choked on it. She felt herself returning to greater awareness. She helplessly fought to retain the unconscious state into which she had, but moments before, been slipping. At least, while closed in by complete blackness, she had been temporarily relieved of the pain.

"Pleeeeease!" Marta whined; her voice sounded like a siren running down. Her head fell forward on her neck. For a brief instant, she saw the blood-smeared steel sticking free of her creamy jug. She puked green and red bile over her tits. The mess drooled down and over belly.

"Names?" Saber insisted. He now hoped that she *wouldn't* give the names—not yet. Even if she did, he didn't know whether or not he'd stop what he was doing. After all, Josef and Karl had had their fun. It was now the Colonel's turn.

Names? Marta wondered *what* names. Who was *she*, for that matter? Who was this smirking man dressed in black? Why couldn't she move her arms or legs? Why was she sick to her stomach? Why did she ache? What was that wicked looking thing peaked through the flesh of her right breast?

Colonel Saber took the second metal hook, suspended from its chain at the opposite end of the bar. He hefted the bulk of Marta's left tit with his left hand. He put the barbed point to the juncture of the tit and the woman's ribcage. He exerted pressure. The hook punctured the flesh. An oozing of new blood exited the puncture, streamed down the woman's belly and disappeared amid the blood and puke-smeared hair at Marta's crotch.

Marta passed out, dropping into welcomed oblivion. She smelled the fumes of another smashed ampoule and actually managed—momentarily—to resist the drug's efforts to revive her. It was so peaceful in the void into which she'd successfully slipped. Was death as peaceful?

Colonel Saber remained diligent in his efforts to bring the girl around. He'd had enough experience to know that, even if the young woman thought she had reached the limits of her endurance, she was wrong. In the end, his efforts were rewarded.

Marta's eyelids fluttered and then shot open to reveal her glassy stare. Her pupils were dilated. She choked on the last remaining ampoule-released fumes.

"How nice of you to decide to rejoin the party," Colonel Saber said, smiling. "We really missed you, there, for awhile."

Marta, her chin drooped, could see the barbs poked through both tits. He'd double-gaffed her like two fisherman landing a tuna.

Oh, why couldn't she just die?

"Handcuff her hands, Karl," Colonel Saber said.

Karl unfastened the pair of cuffs from his belt loop and proceeded to do as he'd been told. He cuffed Marta's hands behind her back and, then, released all support.

For long, uncountable seconds, Marta felt the weight of her upper body supported only by the two hooks stuck through her jugs. Her punctured mammary tissue began to rip. She screamed. She screamed again.

Josef, by the wall, gave more slack to the rope. Marta was allowed to collapse from sitting position to supine. She fell back onto her bound hands, smashing them beneath her. The chains went to piles of collapsed metal links on her shoulders. The metal bar came to rest on her neck, tipping to one side as it did so. The metal, as the end touched the floor, echoed a metallic noise.

Colonel Saber had temporarily ceased his interrogation. He had personal needs that needed satisfying. He began unbuttoning the fly of his uniform trousers.

Karl took his cue. He walked around the Colonel and the girl to Marta's feet. He squatted and took hold of Marta's ankles.

Colonel Saber pulled his cock and accompanying balls from his uniform. His was a big and powerful cock, glutted with blood, slippery with its pre-cum goo. Its corona was completely shot free of its foreskin. The excess skin had become a mass of wrinkled turtle-necking around the flaring edge of the glans. The cock meatus was long, deep, and slightly off-center. The hole was pink, beaded with a pooling of translucent juice. The cock neck was latticed with large and twisting veins that trailed blue lines along the otherwise startling whiteness of

the cock shaft like dark ivy about the thick trunk of
a tree.

At the base of the Colonel's cock roots, sprout-
ing free of his trouser fly, was a bushing of trimmed
and neatly clipped pubic hair. The Colonel's bull-
like balls were shaved hairless.

Saber maneuvered his legs in between Marta's
thighs. Karl, at the girl's ankles, pulled Marta's legs
apart. Simultaneously, he kept her from kicking, although Karl didn't think Marta much up to kicking,
when you came right down to it.

Marta's hands were a cannon ball under her
back. Her arms were elongated bumps on which she
was forced to lie. Her head was forced back on her
neck. Her neck muscles were taut. Her tits were two
mounds on fire.

With a small grunt, Colonel Saber fisted the
white shaft of his cock. He positioned his cock head
to the velvety divide of Marta's pussy.

Marta was so caught up in her world of pain that
she was completely unaware when Saber's cock
drove deeply inside her.

Karl continued to hold Marta's legs secure at the
woman's ankles. He kept Marta's thighs open until
Saber's cock was in full-depth. Then, as if Marta's
legs were the handles of a human nutcracker, Karl
brought them together, clamping cunt around Saber's submerged hard cock. Saber adjusted by lifting his one leg and then the other, dropping them to
the outside of Marta's body. When finished, Saber's
cock was still inside the girl, but he held Marta's
lower body entrapped within the vise made by his
own muscular thighs.

Karl really couldn't understand what pleasure his Colonel could get out of fucking the Jew bitch in her present condition. She was obviously almost dead. Karl preferred his fucks to have a bit more life in them. But, then, this scene always seemed to be just what the Colonel needed to get *his* rocks off. Go figure! Different strokes for different folks.

Marta bucked her hips. The action was more of a spontaneous reflex, spawned by pain, than it was from any pleasure in, or rebellion against, Saber's fucking cock.

Saber curled his hands under the small of Marta's back. He moved his fingers upward. His fingers folded up and over her shoulders near her neck. He held to her, his hips fucking with short, rabbity punches. He enjoyed the way his hard cock moved in her pussy. He liked the way his cock stirred up the female juices and the stale spunk left up her hole by Josef and Karl's previous explosions.

* * * * * * *

MARTA COULDN'T BELIEVE IT when somewhere out of the agony there emerged the faintest flicker of pleasure. She pinched her eyes tightly shut, sure that she'd gone completely mad. What kind of pleasure could she possibly find in any of this?

Saber brought his hips downward, hard. Once again, the man's burgeoning cock rammed home up the pussy. He humped up his hips and then fucked back into her again. Another screwing stroke forced a flood of sticky juice out of Marta's crack. The mess wet Saber's smooth balls and turned his trousers crotch dark with moisture.

Marta smelled of stale sex and blood. The aroma was an aphrodisiac to the man. It made Saber pump his turgid penis even faster. He felt the sharp jolt of electricity tingling his manhood from its glans to its roots.

Colonel Saber screwed Marta for all he was worth. From the sidelines, Josef watched, awaiting his cue.

Karl now stood to one side. He busily rubbed the bulge his hard-on made beneath his trousers. Maybe fucking the bitch, now, wasn't such a bad idea after all. At least, it would be something. Even a half dead Jewess pig could probably get Karl's cock, in its present state of excitement, to let loose its load.

Marta somehow realized she was being fucked. The realization came to her on a breath of ecstasy more and more evident within her hurricane of pain. Yes, there was cock in her crotch. The cock neck rubbed her tender clitoris. The thick cock column massaged her pussy lips, those same pussy lips previously made raw by the slicing mutilations of the Colonel's knife blade. Pulpy cock glans battered every inch of her guts.

Saber's heavy hips again mashed against Marta's cunt. His heavy chest again crushed the girl beneath it. His face burrowed into the sweaty cleavage formed by Marta's hooked jugs. The mammary crease was stained with blood; the smell was sweet to Saber's nostrils.

The rising heat within Marta's cunt made Marta's hips move automatically. The responding movement had nothing to do with any impulses received from her brain. These were received from some more primitive nerve center within her. Somewhere, somehow, a surging of new life came into her body, spawned by the pleasure taking root up her cunt. For Marta who had, just moments before, thought herself blessedly near death, this reprieve wasn't welcome.

Saber pulled his cock out until the ridge around its glans tugged at the mouth of Marta's vagina.

Marta helplessly sobbed. Every new glide of Saber's hard meat against her cervix brought her back farther from the brink of death. Marta resented the return. She didn't want to come back. She wanted the eternal peace that death would give her. Why was she being betrayed by her female body?

Colonel Saber was all the way in Marta's cunt—again. The sheer force of his entering thick prick had concaved the young woman's cunt sleeve. Her ass had begun additional responses, moving now in small circles. All Jew bitches were alike. No matter what the circumstances, they loved cock. They absolutely idolized it. That was probably why it was so hard to stamp out the bastard Jews. They fucked like rabbits, pregnant wombs constantly spewing out their deluge of inferior beings to populate the world.

* * * * * * *

THE SWELLING PLEASURE in her belly ballooned farther. Marta rocked atop her arms and bound hands. Her nipples chafed on the coarse material of the Colonel's uniform. Her belly was scratched raw. Her in-movement butt was ground against the hard floor.

Marta was sweating. The salty oozing poured into the opened wounds made by the whipping she had received upon her first introduction to Colonel Saber. How many hours ago had that been? It seemed an eternity.

Mata's cunt oozed more juice. Her inner thighs were flooded with a new running of fluid each time Saber's cock pumped out of the sexual slot.

Marta was breathing heavily. She was more and more aware of the piston dick within her cunt mouth. She was furious as to how the fucking wasn't *just* painful. It should have been *all* painful! Saber was not a tender lover. He was a sadistic rapist. He was battering Marta's cunt with his cock not to give her even a modicum of pleasure, but because he used her pussy sleeve merely to jack off his swollen Nazi penis.

Saber had pretty much reached fever pitch. His body was soaked with his sweat, on the inside of his uniform, and with Marta's blood and sweat, on the outside.

It wouldn't be long now before Marta pussy thoroughly ruptured the Colonel's nuts. Saber knew that. Anticipating his orgasmic finale only got him hotter. As a direct result, he pumped harder. He drove his cock up Marta's crack like an army battering down the doors of an enemy castle.

"Pig!" Saber grunted. "Goddamned, fucking, Jewess, pig!"

Josef waited by the wall and knew it wouldn't be long now. He nodded for Karl to join him.

On the walk over, Karl continued, with one hand, to massage his cock bulged within his pants. He put his free hand to the rope already held by Josef.

Saber was really caught up in the fuck. He pumped totally out of control, having forgotten what the two soldiers and Marta, were doing in the room with him—except as assumed instruments purely to satiate his own building lust. His cock humped faster. His meat swelled larger. His scrotum contracted to such possessive snugness around his testicles that the curvature of each nut became well-defined witness to the ocean of cum awaiting within for spurted pearly release.

"Pig sticking!" Saber grunted. "I'm...fucking...a...goddamned...pig! Sticking it...sticking it...sticking it!"

Karl quit playing with his bulged erection, both of his hands now devoted to the rope. Joseph and he pulled down. The bar on the other end of the rope, as a direct result, was lifted off Marta's neck, the chains went taut, and the hooks lifted Marta by her tits.

Saber continued fucking, holding on for dear life. His arms clamped hard along the young woman's back. His fingers squeezed Marta's shoulders.

Karl and Josef kept pulling. They elevated Marta completely off the floor. Saber went along for the ride. The Colonel and his victim were both suspended by the hooks anchored in and through Marta's ripping tits.

Saber wrapped his legs around Marta, his cock continuing to deliver penetrating punches to the woman's groin.

"Aaaaoooeoeiiiiii!" Marta screamed. There was no longer any pleasure left for her. The pain was back in multiple denominations. There wasn't a piece of her that wasn't pulsing with agony. The tissues in her breasts ripped farther. More blood oozed the puncture wounds. She didn't even feel Saber's hard cock jettisoning his warm sperm deep into her guts. She didn't even feel the warm-wet wash of hot-milk ocean that basted her pussy membranes and draped them with opaque strings of Nazi cum.

Saber, though, felt his pleasure in a big way. He hung to Marta's suspended body like a greedy monkey to a rare bunch of bananas. His hands and arms clung to her swinging form. His legs scissored just below her butt. His cock poked deep up her cunt and continued coughing up his spermal load.

Josef and Karl maintained their weight to the other end of the rope, keeping Marta and Saber lifted. They held tightly, waiting for their Colonel to finish depositing his cum up the undeserving receptacle.

Even after Saber did finally finish, however, he continued to enjoy the slow swing of Marta and his bodies. Finally, reluctantly, he unhooked his legs and dropped to the floor. His fat cock popped free of the pussy and dragged with it a pink mixture of Saber, Karl, and Josef's spent cum, mingled with Marta's blood. The mess ran the insides of Marta's thighs.

Saber wobbled. He didn't bother stuffing his cock or his balls immediately back into his pants.

He wanted the Jewish whore to take a good look at the phallic weapon that had just provided such fierce cummy cannon-shots so deeply within her. It was an honor she doubtlessly couldn't appreciate fully, but it was an honor for her nevertheless to have had untainted German prick, Saber's untainted German prick, rammed up her tainted Jewish pussy.

With Saber's weight removed from the one end of the rope, Karl and Josef easily managed to tie off their end to a convenient attending wall bracket. When the two soldiers finally let go, they left Marta hanging by the two hooks. Her feet not touching the floor, Marta swung in a nonexistent breeze. Her head was bowed. She looked dead. However, Saber knew she wasn't. Marta, after all, wasn't the first Jewess to swing, thus, from this ceiling. Saber had a wealth of past experience on which to draw.

* * * * * * *

BEFORE REVIVING HER, Saber returned to the cabinet from where he'd originally gotten the hooks. He fished a different drawer. He retrieved a different hook, this one smaller than its predecessors. It was about three inches across its curve. Its handle, a wood dowel, was attached at a right angle. Under different circumstances, it might have been used on farms for shifting bales of hay, or on the docks for moving wood crates. The sweat-darkened grip fit securely in the palm of Saber's right hand. The hook projected between the fore- and fuckfinger of his fist.

Saber walked to Marta's still swaying body and gave instructions to Karl and Josef who stood attendance.

"Revive the whore!" Saber's tensions momentarily assuaged, he was back to business. "Use the hose."

He stepped out of the way. His uniform was a mess. He was filthy and funky. His cock was a drooped rope of slimed flesh. He could use a bath, a nice hot one in which he could soak at length. This had been a grueling afternoon, and Saber was suddenly looking forward to it ending.

The hose, attached to a water outlet at the base of one wall, coiled into a convenient niche when not in use. Josef unwound the hose and aimed its metal nozzle in Marta's direction.

The room was adapted for the equipment used in it. Its floor was a gentle concave centered by a round drain. Any water flowed to hole and left behind cement only damp in aftermath.

Saber nodded. Josef took firm hold of the hose near its nozzle. Karl turned the valve to feed it water.

The result was fire-hose like, although without the same massive volume of released water. A fire hose would have required more than one man to control it, while Josef easily kept this stream of water aimed where it was supposed to go. Still, the water, when and where it spewed, did so under considerable pressure.

"Not at her head, either" Saber reminded. There had been an unfortunate accident wherein gushing water had inadvertently broken one bitch's neck. She'd died without telling Saber what he wanted to know. It could have been a very bad blot on his service record. Luckily, there had been a back-up Jewess more obliging when she'd seen what she could look forward to if she didn't spill her guts.

Within her welcomed cocoon of darkness, Marta heard and felt the unwanted wet summons that insisted she return to the bleak reality. It was as if she were stuck in a washing machine run amuck. A freezing punch to her belly took her breath way. She opened her mouth to gasp for breath. She choked on chilly liquid just before her hooked breasts, her belly, and her crotch were whacked by seemingly icy fists.

Josef expertly drenched her. He aimed the spray up her left leg, over her belly, to her tits, to her belly, to her right leg. He centered in and concentrated the deluge to her cunt. The force of the water rocked Marta on the hooks.

The flushing washed away cum, blood, and dried sweat. The dissolved results flowed the floor to form the man-made vortex that disappeared into the drain.

* * * * * * *

SABER MOTIONED KARL to shut off the water. He had no desire to prolong this any longer. At another time, they might have squirted up her cunt, to one or more orgasms, or stuck the nozzle deeply up her ass, by way of water-hose enema; but not now. Saber's week had been a busy one, and he was tired; he wanted his hot bath. He was losing his patience. These Jews were such fucking goddamned animals. Calling them pigs was a misnomer. They were stubborn jackasses, pure and simple.

Josef wasn't disappointed when the water dribbled to nothing, like tardy cum from a big dick after massive ejaculation. Some guys got turned on by hosing down Jew cunts. Not Josef. Why use a rubber hose to fill up the animals when you could better stuff them with his big Nazi schlong?

"Conscious again, are we, Marta?" Saber asked. He came in from the sideline, walking carefully. He had no intentions of slipping on the damp cement.

Conscious? Was that what Marta was? There was so much pain. Would it ever end?

"I'm tiring of your reluctance to cooperate," Saber warned.

Marta could see him. She was acutely aware of the blackness of his uniform. The material contrasted with the shiny-bright metal hook projected like part of Saber's right hand.

"I want those names, whore," Saber said. He brought the hook up before Marta's face, just in case her numb jackass brain hadn't yet registered it was there. "I want those names, and I want them quickly."

Why shouldn't Marta tell him? Oh, she'd promised she wouldn't, hadn't she? But other people had promised the same, and they'd talked. Marta was here now, being tortured, just because someone, who shouldn't have, had talked. Someone else would talk, whether Marta talked now or not. It was all futile; no matter what her father had so often told her.

"They're out to kill us all, Marta," her father had said. "They are out to kill *each and every* Jew. They will, too, if we don't stop them. In order to stop them, we must live. How can we live if we are continually betraying and betrayed by our own kind?"

But for Marta, here and now, wasn't death better than living? At the time her father had asked her his question, she'd had another answer. Of course, death wasn't preferable to life. That was then; this was now. Now, Marta would welcome death. How wonderful, even, to find refuge within it, no longer any pain.

Saber put the point of the hook to Marta's neck. Where it touched, it punctured the skin and immediately summoned seeping blood.

He drew the point down between Marta's hooked tits as far as her belly. A thin slicing of flesh followed in the point's wake. The blood drained like sap from a maple tree and filled the young woman's navel, overflowed into her cunt hair, and dribbled her thighs.

Saber turned his hook-extended hand, heel up. The metal, now curved back toward his wrist, burrowed the crease of her cunt and nestled within her guarding pubic hair.

The cold metal suddenly against Marta's clitoris sent cold electric shocks throughout the woman's torture-wracked body. The idea of that hook, down there, in her most private place, produced shiver after shiver. Where was the hook's point? Now benign, what if…?

Saber nudged the hook deeper. The leading curve of metal hardness became more and more swallowed by pussy-warmth. But that warmth didn't warm the coldness of the entering steel.

Marta's mouth fell open at the increasing danger entering her twat. Dear God, it was inside of her and slipping ever deeper.

Finally, Saber had almost all of it completely wedged inside her snatch, only the handle left free. His eyes gleamed brightly.

Karl watched and leaned his muscled butt more securely against a table. His hand rested, palm-down, over the bulge his swollen dick made beneath his pants leg. His material-concealed cock drooled moisture to soak the cloth and make sticky the hair on his supporting thigh.

Saber's cock thickened. Still hanging free of his pants, it gave little jerks as it moved from flaccid to bulky.

"Names?" Saber repeated. His hand came back and up to aggressively latch the hook into the roof of Marta's cunt. Raw-red flesh yielded, enfolded, and swallowed.

"They're out to kill us," Marta's father had said. "They're out to exterminate each and every one of us like rats in a cellar."

Saber jerked his right hand again to be sure the hook point was securely anchored in his victim's cuntal wall.

The leading point of the hook sewed all of the way through Marta's hair-grown lower belly. Blood was the crimson thread that came with it.

Oh, God...Oh, God...Oh, God! Marta hadn't a clue how He could allow any of this to happen—to her—to her people—to God's chosen people? Where in the fuck was He? Where in the shit had He always been when the Jews, when a specific Jew, needed Him?

"You will tell us what we want to know," Saber assured. He gave another jerk of the embedded hook that pulled her closer to him. Her dangled legs jerked fish-out-of-water. Her steel-threaded flesh began to tear.

She screamed. She screamed again.

She told him what he wanted to know.

SS & M, by William Maltese

CHAPTER TWO

MEGAN HAD NEVER SEEN A COCK before this cock, not even her father's cock. That wasn't unusual, since she'd lived a relatively sheltered life. Both she and her sister, Marta, had had few boy friends with whom to do sexual exploration. She had early accepted this lack of male suitors when she'd learned, via a long talk with her parents, that she couldn't date regular German boys, because she was a German Jew. She couldn't date Jews, because—for seemingly ever-so-long, the family had masqueraded as non-Jewish German—dating Jews would have called attention to her and her family.

Megan wouldn't be seeing Max's cock if the world hadn't suddenly been turned so upside-down. If her parents knew their teenage daughter was now seeing what she was seeing (even if the cock belonged to a Jewish teenage boy), they would insist Megan join them, despite the danger in her doing so. In life's present nightmare, keeping the family together was usually best achieved by keeping it apart. One night-raid by the Gestapo, and a whole genealogical line could be extinguished forever, if one weren't careful. There was a chance, if only a very slim one, that at least one family member, separately squirreled away, like Megan, might survive the holocaust.

Megan was with the Bruenings—although they weren't really Bruenings. They had some long-concealed Jewish name that Megan didn't know. Why else had they volunteered their attic as sanctuary to Megan and this big-cock Mueller boy—if Max's last name was really Mueller? More likely, it was Minski.

Megan kept her head pretty much covered by goose-down quilt. She pretended sleep.

At sixteen, Max had reached sexual maturity. His balls had long ago dropped. He had hair under his arms, at his crotch, around his knotted belly button, with traces of fur along the small valley between his pectoral muscles and along the deep crease of his firm young ass. He'd masturbated for years and had been helpless to stop when brought to this attic room, albeit doing so only after Megan obligingly went to sleep.

Quite daringly, he usually beat off above-covers. He liked the freedom afforded by his cock fully exposed. He liked to see what he was doing. If the girl showed even the slightest signs of coming awake, it would be easy enough for him to cover up before she realized what was happening on his bed, across the room from her. Megan was such an innocent, Max doubted she even had a clue what jacking-off entailed, or what the cummy results thereof.

Max had a nice cock. It wasn't so large that it would scare off any girl; it wasn't so small that he'd ever been ashamed to remove his pants and underpants in any locker room. As cocks went, and Max had compared his with the ones had by most of his male classmates, his meat was well above average in length and bulk.

He fingered his prick in the moonlight filtered through a dirty skylight. The cool lunar illumination allowed him—and Megan—an uninterrupted view of his healthy cream-white penis.

Max's cock was circumcised. The first time he'd stripped in school, he'd been surprised by how many of his classmates' cocks tapered into elephant snouts. That was the first time he'd had the epithet Jew thrown at him. The name-calling had actually been in jest, at the time, because no one had suspected, then, that Max really was a Jew. Hell, not even Max had known. It was just that any circumcised penis (*mutilated meat,* was how it was referred to by uncut German youth), was always made fun of. In that particular instance, Kurt Shoenbert (whose dick wasn't nearly as big but was just as cut), came to Max's aid. The two beat the shit out of their name-calling classmate. Kurt's father was, after all, even then, a high official in the Nazi party; father and son's cocks clipped for hygienic purposes. Hygienic purposes were, also, the reason Max and his parents always gave for the clipped dicks in their family.

Max fingered his mutilated meat. It looked a lot neater and more streamlined than most of the German sausage hung between pure-blood blond-haired thighs. Max bet even a German-Youth girl would prefer his cock rammed up her belly than take on one of those sock-like cocks with all their interfering extra skin. Max would have liked to verify that suspicion. Much to his dismay, though, his cock had yet to be up any cunt—Jewish, German-Youth, or otherwise—except, of course, in his vivid imagination. He'd almost gotten into Klara Teichmann's pussy, in the garage at her house, but Klara's parents came home early. Klara was now probably damned overjoyed that she'd missed out, most everyone knowing the whole "Mueller" family had turned out to be Jewish swine.

Max hated being a Jew. He would have preferred living in utter ignorance of his heritage, but his father had had to tell him. What a goddamned thing was it to tell your son that he was Jew at the very time anyone Jewish was less desirable to the ruling class than was horse shit still found on some city streets? If his father had for so long been such a lapsed Jew, even to the point of feigning being pure-blooded German, then why in the hell hadn't he just carried on with that charade, instead of screwing up his son's life with the truth? Or…if Max's shitty father had suddenly wanted to go back to being a true Jew, why hadn't he left Germany, and taken his family with him, when the getting was still good? He had had the chance to leave. Instead, he'd stayed. Why? Because, there were profits to be made, after all, in Germany's Jew-hating war economy (what could be more Jewish than that?); Franz Mueller was a Jewish businessman, through and through. Well, he'd made a bundle all right, but he'd stuck around way too long doing it. Where in the fuck were he and his money now? Answer: they were in Nazi hands and pockets. If Max hadn't been staying at friends, the night the black cars came, he, too, would now, this very minute, be suffering in some stink hole with his father and mother—or, more likely, suffering all alone.

He stroked his cock more vigorously, hoping the resulting pleasure would take his mind off those other things. He had loved his mother and father, even if they had tried a dangerous game of deception and failed miserably in the trying. He still loved them, for that matter; it was difficult not to find him caught up in macabre thoughts of what might possibly be happening to them at Gestapo hands.

His fist slid his cock neck, from his hairy lower belly to his bare cock's tip. His dick was pried up so that its pulpy corona aimed directly at a ceiling beam. He tugged what was left of his cock's loose skin, up and down, up and down, around his solid inner cock core.

His cock head was heart-shaped and pink as any valentine. It topped his cock neck that was lightly veined except for the one pronounced run of blue that visibly and impressively meandered from his circumcision scar to his hair-sprouting cock root.

The fuzz on his large balls was the same color as the hair on his head. Certainly it wasn't black, like Jewish hair. His nose wasn't large, or beaked, like Jewish nose. His skin wasn't swarthy, like Jewish skin. In fact, he had none of those subhuman characteristics so often pointed out in laboratories and classrooms. He looked all pure-blood German. His father looked pure-blood German. His mother looked pure-blood German. No wonder, it had initially been so very easy for the Mueller's family to become assimilated into the pure-blood German Aryan community. Even now, after all that had happened, Max, more often than not, simply refused to believe he was Jewish. He still thought it was some kind of mad, rude, and unfair joke someone was playing on him.

So what that there were, among the family heir-looms, that old metal chalice, two small black caps, and a few other things not even Max's father could remember the what or what-for? Where was all that Jewish junk now? Answer: the Gestapo found it. The Gestapo was very thorough when conducting searches of suspect homes. Some black-uniformed black-booted Gestapo had probably already made one or both of Max's parents piss in the chalice and wipe soiled arse or arses on those little black caps.

Max didn't enjoy being cooped up in this attic while all of his non-Jewish peers still enjoyed the comforts of their own homes, the comforts of their own beds. Some of them were probably even getting the comforts of their cocks warmed all nice and toasty up hot and eager pussy, too. Max definitely envied them that.

He continued to stroke his cock, progressing to a harder and faster whipping. He wanted and needed the increased masturbatory friction to take his mind off his disturbing thoughts. He wanted and needed the temporary forgetfulness found within the throes of an orgasm, but stroking his meat to climax took more time, these days; he was no longer the rank amateur who could once cream at the mere touch of his hand.

The truth was, he didn't feel Jewish and never had. He felt pure-blood German. Nor did he want to be a Jew. He wanted to be a Nazi, like all of his friends were probably, by now, Nazis. He wanted to wear the sexy black uniform and sexy black boots with the sexy lightning-bolt SS insignias. He'd even, at times, imagined himself interrogating members of the Jewish subhuman species—those fantasies continuing, even after he'd found himself suddenly one of that piggy sub-group.

Megan continued to be fascinated by what she saw. It was hard to believe that the stiff appendage, jutting at its impressive right angle from Max's body, was actually a physical part of the boy. Seeing his hard dick made Megan feel all funny inside, like she sometimes did when she played with herself; her sister Marta had taught her how to gently manipulate her tiny clitoris. And where was Marta now? They had picked her up in one of their black cars. They had taken her away like they seemed to be taking away everyone nowadays. Megan wondered if she'd ever see her sister again—or see her father, or her mother.

At that moment, however, it was preferable to exchange such miss-her-family emotionally draining thoughts for thoughts of Max's cock and what he was doing with and to it. Megan fascinated by all of Max's revealed and virile nakedness. It was all so new and exciting. Her pussy oozed warm buttery juices because of it. The stickiness wet the insides of her thighs. She wanted to touch herself down there, but she couldn't risk it. If Max saw any movement from her, he might stop. Or, maybe he'd cover up and carry on underneath the covers. Neither of which Megan would like.

Max was finally getting where he wanted to be. His persistent pumping had finally turned his cock into a hot poker in his fisted hand. The heat had finally spiraled from his beaten prick into the rest of his body. He was finally beginning to feel good, really good. He knew he would soon—finally—be feeling even better.

His caressing hand moved so fast now—up and down, up and down, the length of his stiff meat—his fist and cock appeared blurred by the motion. He tightened the muscles of his ass, and his butt literally lifted from the mattress.

* * * * * * *

MAX FANTASIZED, which always made masturbation better. He imagined himself a member of the elite *Schutzstaffel,* in his black uniform, complete with his polished black boots. He was in the cellar of Gestapo headquarters. He had just walked into one cubicle to see the young and innocent Jewish girl he intended to make his sex slave, and make her like it.

"Suck my cock, bitch!" he commanded. Like the slave she was, she opened her mouth and sucked his privates all of the way to Max's fat balls.

Did the Gestapo have Max's mother, at that moment, in just such a cell? Was some fat slob in a black uniform and black boots, his pants open, forcing Max's mother's face down and over a hugely erect pure-blood German cock? That thought suddenly made Max's pleasure pale considerably. He even quit pumping his cock. Simultaneously, he suspected Megan wasn't asleep but watching.

Though he didn't follow through, his immediate response was to cover himself. What would have been the point of doing that, at this late date, though? Something about—shutting the cage door after the anaconda had already gotten out. Besides, there was nothing wrong with what he was doing. A healthy guy had to get his rocks off some time, somehow, somewhere, or they'd turn blue and fall off.

"You *are* awake, aren't you, Megan?" Max interrogated her from his side of the room. His hand gave a languid stroke of his seemingly even harder pecker. His cock meatus drooled juice that the heel of his thumb spread, like clear syrup, over the surface of his pulpy cock head.

Megan didn't answer, only feigned continued sleep. How could he know she was awake, anyway? She'd tried so hard to be silent. She hadn't moved a muscle. He had to be guessing.

He got to his feet. He walked the distance to Megan on her mattress, his wobbling hard cock leading the way. His balls swung like pendulums from the base of his stiff dick.

"I know you're awake, Megan" he said.

She didn't answer. She was embarrassed. She was mortified! How could she have watched him playing with himself? How could he have found her out? How could she now own up to being awake the whole time? She wanted, simply, to curl up in a little ball, beneath her covers, and disappear.

"You want me to stick my hard cock up your pussy?" Max asked. If he hadn't been really certain she was awake, he was certain now. He could see where one bit of her quilt was lifted for peeking.

Megan didn't say anything. She realized suddenly she was holding her breath.

"You have a virgin cunt?" Max asked. What would he do if Megan started screaming rape? That would be dangerous, but did Megan realize just how dangerous?

Hell, maybe he would rape her. Certainly, he'd raped more than his share of women in his fantasies. He'd raped them really well, too. Here was his chance to taste the real thing. He'd throw back this little Peeping Cunt's quilt, hop on her bones, and put his willie up her virgin twat. And, who would come to her rescue? The Bruenings, that's who! If she screamed, they would come running. Max could say she'd had a nightmare. Would the Bruenings believe that, Megan's virgin blood on his cock and on her bed by way of contradiction?

"Just continue watching, then, cunt. I'll show you what you're missing out on. I've man-cock here, good as it is stiff. It's all yours for the asking. Should you change your mind, just jump on in and say so."

Megan was frightened. Megan was excited. Megan's cunt leaked gallons of liquid that soaked her blankets and her with it. She was hot. She was bothered. She was sweating. She could hardly swallow.

Max took a wider stance. He thrust his hips forward. He took a firm hold of his cock with his right hand. He was back in his black uniform and black boots. He was back in Gestapo headquarters. He was back in the cellar, having opened that cell door to the young and innocent victim he now knew was little Jewess Megan Steiger, soon to be down on her hands and knees, crawling toward him, her tongue obscenely licking her lips and, then, obscenely licking his big pure-bred Nazi dick. She had such succulent pink lips, just made for sucking.

"Want to chew on some genuinely pure-blood German cock, Jew, bitch?" Max asked. Megan's eyes went wide. "It's all yours, slut. Have at it whenever you're ready!"

Max pumped his hard cock in earnest. Simultaneously, he twisted his gliding fist around the shaft of his prick as he imagined his cock wrung of its juices by Megan's tightly squeezing virgin pussy. He cupped his free hand beneath his balls and rolled his nuts in their containing bag of contracting scrotal flesh.

"Yeah, baby, lick my nuts," Max grunted. He shut his eyes. He revolved his hips. He fucked his hand.

Megan didn't know what was happening, but it was the most exciting thing that ever had happened to her: Max standing there, so close that Megan could have sat up and touched the boy's manhandled cock. Megan who had never before seen a naked boy or naked cock, was seeing both, right here and now, and undeniably enjoying the seeing like crazy; Max playing with himself. Max yanking his pud and saying filthy, cruel, mean things.

"You want it, honey," Max grunted; it wasn't a question. "You want it. I know you do."

The simple truth was that Megan *did* want it. She did want Max's hard cock. Her pussy wanted it, too. Wasn't that why her cunt was sopped with warm juices? Would she ever get another chance like this one? How did she know what tomorrow would bring? Maybe, the police would come for her. Maybe they'd even be there, within minutes, to kill her in a blast of gun fire. Would Megan die a virgin? Would she know the wonder of hard cock up her cunt? Time suddenly too precious to waste. It was all right to be a prim, proper, and modest little Jewish girl when she had years and years ahead of her. What, though, if she only had a few remaining minutes? Was that what Max tried to tell her in his unique and sordid way?

"My cock wants you," Max said. His ass muscles dimpled with each forward rocking of his hips to put his cock, again and again, into his fictitious victim's (into Megan's) willing face.

* * * * * * *

AS IF HYPNOTIZED INTO COMPLI- ANCE, by the movement of Max's hand over Max's cock, Megan pushed herself free of her quilt. She pulled her night gown above her waist, baring her cunt. The cool air of the attic made Megan shiver as it bathed her nakedness. She shut her eyes.

"Yes," she whispered. "Yes...yes...yes...I *do* want it."

Hearing her voice, Max opened his eyes. Megan lying there, half naked, in open invitation, made his masturbatory fist skip a beat. He almost creamed, right then and there. She looked so lovely, so inviting. Her sparsely haired cunt looked so deliciously fuckable. Max's cock was drawn to that pussy like an iron filing drawn to a magnet.

"We don't have much time," Megan whispered. Her eyes were clenched tightly, but she knew Max saw what she blatantly and shamelessly revealed for his viewing and fucking pleasure. His hungry gaze ate into her like acid into metal. "They will be here soon."

They could be there soon, too. They came at night. They hauled away mothers, fathers, sisters, brothers, aunts, uncles, cousins, nieces, nephews, lovers, and friends. They deposited one and all in the back of vans, then into dark rooms at Gestapo headquarters. That was the last anyone ever saw of them. They could drop both Max and Megan just as easily into some deep and dark hole and leave them there forever. God, but Megan didn't want to die a virgin.

"We *will,* you know?" Marta had often told Megan in the privacy of their own room—when they'd had a room, when they'd had a house, when they'd had parents downstairs. "We'll both die virgins just because our father is so money hungry he stays on in Germany, masquerading as a true Aryan, just to put a few extra coins in his coffers. What good will all his fine talk of dowries do you and me if we're found out? We're Jews trapped inside a Germany that more and more hates its Jews."

"Hurry," Megan whispered to Max. Her hands roamed her thighs, inward and down toward her awaiting cuntie. The slipperiness of her love juices was smooth and oily against her exploring fingertips.

"Yes," Max said. His voice was breathless. "Yes, by God, yes."

His suddenly weak legs collapsed him, hard and heavy, without a bit of gracefulness, between Megan's opened legs. He leaned his torso over her. He aimed his hard cock toward the inviting target that was her juice-primed pussy. He shivered with the utter delight of initial touch-down.

"Give it to me!" Megan begged. Her flesh against his sent her into minor orgasm. She really wanted his cock now, not just the pulpy head of it massaging her crease. She not only wanted it, she needed it, had to have it, for her own personal salvation.

With a moan of building passion, Max began to insert the head of his stiff prick through the guardian gateway of Megan's virgin cunt. Her velvety twat lips began to part beneath the increasing press of his cock head. Her hot cuntal wetness oozed by way of greeting.

The anticipatory pleasure, though, proved too much for poor Max who may have become jaded to masturbation, from overindulgence, but had never before been this close to any cunt, especially virgin. Suddenly, his body jerked in apparent seizure. His cock came completely out of alignment with Megan's pussy-slot. A sudden downward misaimed heave of his hips jabbed his prick not into Megan's cunt but in a lengthways slide along its outer groove.

* * * * * * *

"GIVE IT TO ME, "I SAID!" Megan commanded, frankly surprised and disappointed when she didn't have Max fully inside of her as Max had volunteered, boasted, and promised.

Max, unfortunately, was beyond filling anything. His premature ejaculation took complete hold of his senses with a suddenness that chattered his teeth and pointed his toes as his spunk blew off target to soil his belly and hers. His body collapsed hard against her body and ground to an eventual stop within the slippery mess of his own making.

"Goddamn-it!" he grunted, frustrated and disgusted in not having performed as a man, despite the opportunity she'd given him.

It took both several minutes to realize the loud sounds they heard weren't their beating hearts but black uniformed, black-booted Gestapo breaking down the door.

SS & M, BY WILLIAM MALTESE

CHAPTER THREE

SERLE SCHELLING. Lieutenant Schelling. Melissa Schelling. Lieutenant and Mrs. Schelling. Yes, Melissa liked the way those rolled off her tongue. She liked the way they tasted, almost as good as Serle's cock. Not quite, but almost.

She had his cock, now, deep in her throat. When she swallowed, her neck muscles contracted around its shaft and squeezed its pulpy head. Each constriction milked it of more delicious and slightly salty preseminal leakage.

"Mmmmm," Melissa savored her mouthful. Her nose buried deeper into the bush of Serle's blond pubic hair. Her chin rested on the cushion formed by his bull-like, compact, and hairy scrotum. Her hands gently caressed the blond fuzz on his muscular thighs.

By turning her head slightly to the right, she could see their naked bodies reflected in the mirror of the wardrobe closet. She liked what she saw. They made quite an impression, the two of them, hooked together head-to-groin.

Her darker good looks contrasted pleasingly with his tanned blondness. She liked to wear all

white to the opera or ballet. On those formal occa-
sions, he would be in his black *Schutzstaffel* uniform. They always drew appreciative stares. One
lucky night, attending a performance of Wagner's
Siegfried in Berlin, the Führer himself asked who
they were. "The nephew of Baron Natal Schelling
and the nephew's fiancée," Hitler was told. "Exquisite pairing," the Führer had responded.

Melissa soon-to-be-Schelling-nee-Goerman, engaged to marry one of the SS's up and coming
young officers. Life couldn't be better. The Nazi
forces were conquering the world, and her man was
among that Nazi elite. These were thrilling times.
She believed in living them to the limit.

"Easy," Serle whispered instructions, placing a
steadying hand in Melissa's hair, combing gently.
"Slow and easy."

God, how lucky she was. He was so goddamned
beautiful, or was the word handsome? He was *more*
than handsome. The first time she'd met him, just
looking at him had taken her breath away. That his
uncle was a Baron was purely a bonus—a title Serle
would one day inherit. Melissa would be a Baroness. She liked that Baroness idea—very, very much.
She didn't care what her father or mother said. How
could they be so against a match that was so obviously made in heaven that even god Hitler ap-
proved?

Serle's powerful thigh muscles tightened beneath her fingertips. Her lips sucked upward over
the spike that was her man's erect cock. The ridged
section of his flared penis head caught just behind
her lips. She paused. She looked down the long-long
length of hard and spit-shined prick that extended so

impressively between her mouth and his hairy lower belly.

His cock, to Melissa, was a cock just made for her sucking. It and she felt so damned good when she had it all inside of her mouth. It wasn't too big (at least, for her, after much practice), and was a decidedly delectable mouthful. It had good, smooth lines, with no distortion of veins along its shaft. It was golden, its glans slightly darker than its shaft. Its meatus was deep and pouted, exactly centering and twinning the cock corona.

Her face dropped back along the cock. Lovingly, she sucked right to its roots. Serle's blond pubic hair tickled her nose. She giggled over his cock-in-her-mouth. Her vibrating throat muscles massaged his dick. He growled his appreciation.

He groaned again and watched her head make yet another upswing. Helplessly, his hips gave a small bucking movement that tried to reclaim her discarding mouth. Melissa, after some training, gave excellent head. Her ability to learn fast was part of her attraction. Even more of her charm rested within her cunt and ass, because she had learned to give a wicked fuck, no matter in which of her orifices he decided to stick her. Also, she was exceptionally attractive. Everyone, even Hitler, said so.

The couple always drew attention, no matter where or when. That was a good thing when you were in the SS. Sometimes Serle found his uncle's connections not really enough to unlock certain doors. Actually, they could be a hindrance. Hitler, not from the aristocracy, obviously wasn't naturally inclined to be overly attentive to the advancement of the nephew of any Baron. However, the Führer's comments to Himmler at the opera, that one lucky evening in Berlin, had Serle's superiors running to do Serle favors. It was now rumored he was destined for bigger and better "things". He'd already fucked two girls for the sole purpose of breeding. Both were deliriously pregnant. Such fucking privileges made it more than evident that the party thought highly of Serle's intelligence, physicality, and potential.

And all of that had come from just the one evening of Wagner with Melissa. Before that, Serle hadn't met the Führer, let alone talked to him. Before that, he'd merely, been but one more of the awe-struck crowd who gave homage when the Führer passed by in the distance. But now....

Baron Schelling didn't approve of the match but, then, fuck his uncle! These were new times. You couldn't expect rewards any longer just because your family had been in Germany since the Year One. You had to do things on your own. You had to go out and carve out a piece of the world for yourself, not rely on the ill-won accolades thrown your way because of ancestors never seen. And the world, at present, certainly seemed ripe for the carving.

"Ohhhh, shit, easy, easy," Serle grunted. His mind was brought back to the reality by another exceptionally exquisite slide of Melissa's taut lips and tongue over his mouth-and-throat-submerged hard penis.

* * * * * * *

MELISSA CONCENTRATED ON her mouthful. She pulled back up Serle's cock to his cock head. She lapped the bulbous coronal top and siphoned off all of its immediately available saline slickness.

His hands got heavier against her scalp. He pushed her face, once again, over the totality of his swollen penis. His cock head deflected off her palate, slid comfortably into the opening of her throat.

She took all of it, all of the way down, without gagging once; she was so familiar with "the how" of it raking the very back of her gullet.

He held her face down deep over his prick. He liked the feel of her anchored there, his cock in her hugging oral tunnel. He finally released the pressure and, right on cue, her lips slid back up his spit-soaked erection.

She rolled her tongue around his swollen cock glans, her tongue tip lovingly darting into juicy meatus. The length of her tongue curled the belly of his cock by way of slide way for the return of his hard meat inside her.

Using her ears as handles, he guided her face— back and forth, up and down—over his hard penis. His cock felt really good, but, suddenly, it wanted the substituted pleasure and silkier feel of Melissa's cunt.

On the next upward stroke of Melissa's face, Serle pulled it completely free of his dick. His released hard stalk plopped back hard against his bare and muscled belly, splattering a sunburst of spit to the young man's washboard abdominals.

Automatically, she tried to recover his lost dick. He thwarted her.

"No sense in wasting my load up your mouth," he said. "Let's get to some serious baby-making."

Melissa knew he would be delightedly surprised to find out his previously spewed thick seed was already rooted and sprouted in her belly. She had just received the doctor's report that morning. It was to be her little surprise for her love: the dessert to finish off their evening. Serle desperately wanted children to carry on his family name and title. He wanted to be a father. But the surprise of his wishes to come true, sooner than he expected, was information for later. Tell him now that she was pregnant, and he might have been reluctant to fuck her. Men were strangely ignorant, in that they, almost to a one, thought pregnancy meant no more fucking. Did they imagine their frantically plowing cocks would poke holes in the fetus?

She smiled and rolled to her back on the bed. Her pussy wanted his cock as badly as his cock wanted her pussy. She'd let him fuck her senseless, now. Then, resting there, satiated, in the afterglow of hot and heavy sex, each in the other's arms, she'd tell him their good news.

She opened her creamy thighs. His body fell comfortably and familiarly into the space on the bed parenthesized by her legs. His cock head went immediately to the mouth of her buttery cunt. Her vagina juice waited to lubricate the plunge of his dick inside her. Melissa's thrilled in anticipation.

The mouth of her pussy first concaved and then opened wide under the exerted persistent pressure of Serle's cock to attain entrance. Her muscled cunt ring yawned all the more as the ridged crown of

Serle's cock actually pushed through with a re-sounding wet noise.

* * * * * * *

"OHHHHH," MELISSA SIGHED. As often as Serle poked her, every which way from Sunday, she never got enough.

Serle growled against her neck. His teeth scraped the flesh of her throat. His lips nuzzled her cheek. His tongue licked the outline of her ear.

She wiggled within his embrace. His body was so hard against hers. She loved the feel of its athletic build. His pectorals were solid domes of pale golden flesh. The hardness of his punctuating nipples was like tacks against her tits. His scalloped belly was a sexy roughness of ridged flesh against her softer stomach. His cock was a steely shaft jabbed deep into the mushy softness of her eagerly accepting pussy.

His arms hooked beneath her knees. He lifted and butter-flied her thighs on the bed. Her vulva moved even farther as the hugeness of his cock shaft followed his cockhead inside her.

Groaning, she moved her ass, twisting her vagina around his penile plug. His rigid cock was momentarily snagged up her cunt, held securely within her honey-drenched hole. Seconds later, miraculously freed of its complete entrapment, it withdrew to its head.

Melissa's hands rested on Serle's back. The man's body muscles stiffened as he hunched his hips more powerfully. His cock re-nestled within her enfolding twat, with every additional push into her feather-soft but snug vaginal purse.

He kissed her hair. He growled softly as he fucked—in and out, in and out. His plowing dick shifted, and stirred her cuntal membranes. The fullness of his pulsing erection forced its way—back and forth, back and forth...this way, that way, and every which way.

For Melissa, his cock felt unbearably good, doing what it was doing. She grew more ecstatic as her cunt walls were friction-drug inward with his each and every inward thrust within them, and then slid outward with each and every withdrawal of his hard, thick, dick.

"Fuck me...fuck me...ahhhhh, yes...fuck me!" Melissa begged. Her fingers dug his back.

His swollen shaft continued its movements. Melissa's ass responded with circular jerks of excitement. She twisted her hips sideways. The tip of his cock gouged one cuntal wall and then the other. Her lower body bounced—up and down—as he continued pumping, pumping, pumping.

The rub of his cock meat against her clitoris caused her nothing but increased pleasure. Her juices gushed around the edges of her fucked pussy. Her black cunt hair plastered her labia. More of his fucking sucked even more natural lubricant from her vaginal walls to cocoon his cock up her cunt.

Her nipples burned. As if he sensed the itch growing in her tits, he licked her neck to her full-blown jugs. He found one of her roseate nipples. He tongued its taut center. He nuzzled it with his lips. He bit it gently. She thrust her tits upward, hard against his face. Her taut-nippled soft boobs mashed around his burrowing cheeks.

He continued to fuck. His balls swung to smack her upturned ass on each inward thrust. The outside of his scrotum was awash with her flooding cunt juices, his scrotal hair beaded with them.

* * * * * * *

"FEEL GOOD?" SERLE ASKED, and his voice was whispery and breathless. "Is it good for you, baby? Is it as good for you as it is for me?"

"Good, yes!" Melissa grunted. Fucking YES, was it good! It was more than *just* good. It always was.

More throes of ecstasy coursed through her. If they originated at her cunt (which they did), they quickly swept through her thighs and her belly. They turned all of her hot and tingly.

She bucked beneath his fucking. She ground her pelvis against his lower belly. Her lips sought his. Her tongue thrust deeply into his mouth. Pleasure again engulfed her as he sucked her tongue and the faintly his-cock-tainted spit she fed him.

Her clit had long gone rigid. It was a miniature female cock jutted from the folds of her raw-red pussy.

She sensuously swayed her hips. His cock continued to hammer into her.

He panted in her ear, and his prick shoved and withdrew in her cunt. On each new shove, his cock jammed to its roots, and his blond pubic hair tangled with the black bush of her snatch; his cock back pressed and tightly dragged against her throbbing clitty.

The heat from the friction within her cunt seemed to melt Melissa's sexual membranes into oily butter. Nonetheless, her cunt somehow squeezed more tightly over Serle's cock. The fire inside her welled to greater intensity and burned from point of origin to the roots of her hair and the tips of her toes. The inferno increased as her hips swiveled to stir her cunt, mortar-with-penile-pestle, around his heartily pumping penis.

His mouth hurriedly returned to her nipples and landed, occasionally, long enough to playfully bite budded centers. His hands clamped her ass. His lower body jerked upward from the bed. He held her tighter, and his cock rammed harder, faster, and more furious into her sex hole.

His pounding pubic bone bruised her love mound and acted as a masochistic aphrodisiac for her rising sexual hunger. Her heart was an out-of-control drum roll.

She couldn't get enough, fast enough, of his expertly fucking prick. Even though the burgeoning tip of his piston shaft knocked at the very mouth of her womb, she wanted more...more...more. Her hips gyrated more violently, and she shook all over, as if gone spastic or into grand-mal seizure. His cock head, as a direct result, reached its deepest inward shove. Building tension increased for both of them.

She opened her mouth. She gasped for air. Simultaneously, she jabbed her revolving pelvis, again and again, hard, harder into his humping belly. Sexual sounds occurred at impact: loud, slurpy—cock-plowing-pussy-again-and-again-and-again—sounds; cock-out-of-control sounds.

Melissa sensed his impending orgasm. Mentally, she tried to gear her body to join his. Her teeth gritted, and she concentrated all of her remaining willpower into achieving simultaneous orgasm with him.

Once again, the muscled lining of her cunt tightened. Her steaming pussy sleeve was a vise. Her whole body focused on milking frantically the entire length and circumference of Serle's on-the-brink-of-orgasm boner.

"Baby!" he grunted. His body stiffened. His rhythmic fuck strokes ceased. He stopped dead-still with only his cock head securely within the hole between her legs. He was on the verge. He knew it. She knew it. There was no holding back. So, he dropped one final time to insert all of his cock—head to roots—deeply into Melissa's willingly welcoming twat. The resulting heat and friction was simply, finally, too unbearable to endure.

"Feed my hungry cunt!" Melissa commanded. "Oh, sweet mercy, feed it...feed it...feed it."

Serle obliged, actually with no choice, the decision completely out of his conscious control. The resulting meal of spermal mush he fed his fiancée's snatch would have choked a horse.

Melissa felt the long-awaited eruption finally filling her innards. Her pussy walls clenched in hard upon the exploding tube of male meat and massaged the erect cannon. Every muscle in her body contracted, spasmed, jerked. Her hips rocked like a small boat on angry waves. She gasped harder for air. She jabbed her fingernails into Serle's sweaty back and drew blood. She screamed her ecstasy to the rooftop.

The jolting slugs of his cum erupted again... again...again. Each new blast drove Melissa into another sexual crescendo. She was always wondrously surprised by how much spunk Serle's nuts could shoot into her in the course of any one ejaculation. There seemed endless gallons of it.

Serle ceased his orgasmic trembling. His hands unclenched Melissa's ass. He let her butt lower back to the bed. Her cunt muscles, albeit reluctantly, released their stranglehold on his hard cock as he started pulling himself free of her cum-drenched cavity.

Having second thoughts, she tried to stop his cock from a complete withdrawal. She so liked the feel of his penis going soft inside her (she could often orgasm when it did so), her palms now fanned his hard ass cheeks and clamped down to keep him locked in place. His cock slipped free despite her efforts to contain it. His exiting prick trailed a web of sticky spent cum and a cacophony of sticky wet sounds.

Serle rolled to his back on the bed beside her. His cum-soaked dick deflated into more softness along his left thigh. He stretched, and his body's muscles sensuously elongated and then relaxed beneath his bronzed flesh.

Melissa rolled toward him. Her left leg hooked over the nearest of his. Her head laid on one of his muscled and sweaty pectorals, her ear against one of his still-taut nipples. She kissed his skin and savored its sexy taste. Her fingers traced his belly to his damp pubic bush. She combed the wiry-furred blondness of his lower-belly and moved on to fondle his puffy but now almost completely flaccid penis.

He put his hand in her hair and sifted her silky strands though his fingers. He made a low purring sound of obvious male animal contentment.

Earlier, Melissa had decided upon this very moment to tell him of her pregnancy. She would have, too, if she wasn't interrupted by the explosion of splintering wood.

* * * * * * *

SERLE HAD EXCELLENT REFLEXES. Melissa would always remember how quickly he was out of the bed, like a shot, and reaching for his Borchardt-Luger automatic pistol in its holster hung on a nearby chair. And, in the weeks to come, she would recall all of it, more and more. It was the final act of one of their lives, the beginning act of quite another.

There were six of them who barged into the bedroom. They all wore black. Five of them held rifles.

"Lieutenant, put down your gun!" the sixth man ordered Serle, every gun but Serle's gun aimed in Serle's direction.

Melissa knew this sixth man: Lieutenant Johann Stempfle. He was Serle's friend. He was *her* friend. He was dating a pretty young girl, Heidi Dormacher. Melissa liked both of them and had always enjoyed their company.

"What in the hell is this, Johann?" Serle asked. "A joke?" He re-holstered his Luger but made no attempt to cover his nakedness. On the other hand,

Melissa burrowed deeper within all available blankets.

"Lieutenant, a word with you in the other room, please," Stempfle said. His continuing use of formal military address was lost on neither Serle nor Melissa.

"This had better be damned good, Lieutenant," Serle warned in equally military-speak, and reached for his robe.

"Serle?" Melissa asked, expectantly. She didn't know why she had such a premonition of more nastiness to come of all this. She did know she didn't want Serle to leave the room. She didn't want to be left alone with these five men (their guns in and out of their pants). Their presence completely shattered her peaceful, idyllic little world of but minutes before.

"I'll take care of it—whatever *it* is," Serle promised. He fastened the belt of his robe, securing the terry cloth around him. He followed Stempfle into the other room. The door closed behind them.

Alone, except for the five men in black...she naked, except for the sheet and blankets that covered her...Melissa felt a sudden chill down to the very marrow of her bones. How could things have gone from such unadulterated bliss to this, and done so within so short a time? No matter what Searle said, Melissa suspected he wasn't going to take care of anything—whatever *anything* was.

Ten hungry eyes devoured the outline of her body beneath her covers. The men held their weapons so that the black long barrels looked like large Negro cocks jutted from between masculine German thighs. The illusion was as frightening as it was sexual.

What in the fuck was this all about? Why hadn't Johann, and his drooling companions, merely knocked on the door? He'd done just that plenty of times before, and Melissa or Serle had willingly let him in, just as they would have this time. Why barge in like the Gestapo after some smarmy Jew? Why the armed escort? Had Serle done something? Was Melissa's man not whom she thought he was? Was the five-man escort there to take him away? If so, what was it doing standing guard over *her*?

It seemed an eternity for Melissa while she waited. During those long minutes, she only heard the muffled conversation of Serle and Johann through the wall and closed door. On more than one occasion, Serle was shouting.

When the door did open, Melissa could tell by Serle's expression that their world was ending. Even if the five men with guns hadn't been there, or Johann with his still-official air, Melissa could have foretold disaster by the sickly pastiness that had somehow surfaced through Serle's usually healthy tanned skin.

Serle came to the bed. Johann stayed by the door. The other five men stood their ground and remained rooted where they were.

Serle looked down at Melissa. What was there to be read in the angry sparks from his eyes and from the tic, not there before, suddenly in his right cheek?

"Get up!" he commanded her. His voice was strained, a strange octave higher than normal.

"Serle, what is it?" It should have been so different, so very different. By this time, she should have already told him about their baby. The two should have been hugging, kissing...maybe even preparing for another bout of heated sex.

"Get up!" he repeated. His voice had a nasty edge.

What was the matter? Why wouldn't he just tell her what was going on?

She obeyed him, bringing a sheet with her to cover her nakedness. She stood, sheet-draped, before him. He had never appeared to her so big, so powerful...so...so...menacingly Nazi.

"Serle, I..."

He didn't let her finish. He ripped the sheet from her body and left her to stand stark naked. One of her hands reflexively went to shield her tits, the other hand automatically moved to cover her cunt. Helplessly, she blushed deeply pink. If she'd been shameless in her nakedness before Serle, it was entirely different before Johann and five complete strangers.

"You bitch!" Serle accused between clenched teeth. He spit in her face, and the gob splashed slimily on one cheek and immediately drooled. Still, Melissa didn't wipe it away, because concealing the vulnerability of her naked tits and cunt remained her prime objective.

"You filthy Jew!" Serle screamed in her face; she noticed the familiarly distinctive peppermint odor of his breath, caused from the residue of lozenge he'd sucked just before crawling into bed.

She heard what he said. However, it didn't register. How could it? Melissa a Jew! Ridiculous! Impossible! Ludicrous! What kind of cruel joke was being played on her, here? And, who in the hell was playing it? And, why was the love of her life participating in it?

"You goddamned lying Jewish slut!" His fist drove hard into her belly.

Inside of her, accompanied by an explosion of unbearable pain, something once vital was crushed. Simultaneously, she doubled over and rocked backwards. The back of her knees hit the edge of the bed. Her legs gave way.

She tried to scream, but she could only wheeze.

* * * * * * *

THERE WAS A SEARING FLASH of new agony to herald and confirm something fatally damaged inside of Melissa. A gush of pink fluid, another verification, painfully burst from her pussy lips.

"Oh, dear God, our baby!" She recognized the horror even through her accompanying major distress. "Oh, our baby!" she found full voice to scream out at him the reality of the horrible, irreparable, damage he'd done them.

SS & M, BY WILLIAM MALTESE

CHAPTER FOUR

MAJOR PHILLIPP SONNENBURG enjoyed these little excursions into the field. He didn't have to make them. He could have stayed ensconced at headquarters, letting younger men bring the piglets to him. However, he found these little trips stimulating, mentally as well as physically.

He looked at his naked belly reflected in the mirror. Megan's naked body was reflected, too. The soldiers had brought the girl down from the attic. They'd tied her to the bed. They'd left her alone with the Major. Yes, rank had its privileges. Coming out on these forays with the boys, assured him of some prime pickings before they had been worked over.

Take this little Jewish slut for example. Now, she was a prime young piglet. What would have been his chances of getting her once she arrived at headquarters for interrogation? Not very good. Brought in tonight, this one would have fallen to Stahlhelm or Saber. Even, if by chance, Sonnenburg had found out early that she had been picked up, he would have probably found her more than a little used by the time he pulled rank and got to her. He had seen more than a few good pieces of ass ruined before he got his cock into them. After all, just because he outranked Stahlhelm, it didn't mean that the interrogation procedures stopped dead until the Major checked out all the newly arrested Jews and picked out the best ones for personal fucking. Interrogations were to move swiftly, be carried out on a twenty-four-hour basis. That directive had come down from the top. Every second some Jew wasn't naming a fellow conspirator, some Jewish bitch was clandestinely whelping another hunk of subhuman shit in some dark corner of the civilized world.

Out here, however, was another thing. Out here, the Major had precedence over even Colonel Saber.

Oh, he thanked his lucky stars for this evening's little outing. Jews were being smoked out nightly, but it was very seldom a little treasure like this one turned up. Nice and young and virgin. He had hardly believed the evidence of her hymen intact when he'd stuck his finger as far as he could into her tight little cuntie. Miracle of miracles! He'd obviously gotten here just in time. A couple more minutes and that hymen would have fallen victim to the pounding of that Jewish kid's cock. From the spermal mess on the girl's attic mattress, and the Jew-boy's puffy cock, it was more than clear that some kind of sexual fun and games had been in progress even as the Major and his men broke in the door. How tragic it would have been for the Major had he lost out to some bastard Jew boy who had no idea as to what a treasure he was getting.

Sonnenburg pinched the loose flesh hanging as a spare tire around his middle. He was getting flabby. There'd been a time when he couldn't even visualize himself in his present wretched physical state. There was just too much sitting around on his ass and not enough field training. He should try to get out even more with the patrols. The boys in the other room were in damned good shape. They were, however, considerably younger than Sonnenburg's forty-two years.

Then again, all things considered, he wasn't in as bad a shape as some he'd seen his age. He still had a little something left inside of him for this little Jewish Miss.

He lingered a little while longer before the mirror. No matter how good he looked, or didn't look, considering everything, he wished he looked better. His hair was going gray and receding. He had two noticeable liver spots on his right cheek. His eyes looked perpetually wet and, these days, were often watering. He was developing a tic near the corner of his left eye. His chest was turning blubbery. His belly was slack. His legs had lost their muscle tone. Standing naturally and looking down, he couldn't even see his prick or his feet beneath his stomach overhang.

If and when he consciously held in his belly, he saw the salt-and-pepper coloring of his once all-blond pubic bush. Holding in his gut was just too much bother and effort, though. If he really wanted to see his cock and balls, he could, like now, always find a mirror.

If his cock and balls, like the rest of him, weren't what they used to be, just whose cock and balls *were* the same at forty-two as they'd been at twenty-two?

Well, he refused to stand around yearning for years that used to be and would never be again. This was here and now. He had a nice piece of Jewish ass tied to the bed, just waiting for him.

Flaccid, the Major's cock would soon be standing tall. He would soon be fucking cunt; and, it was virgin cunt no less. He hadn't gotten too many of those, even in his prime.

He went to his trousers that he'd folded neatly over the back of a chair. He unthreaded his belt from the pants loops. He folded the belt in on itself. He took both ends in his right hand. He went to the bed. People were waiting for him to finish so they could have their turn. Undoubtedly, they were in the other room now, cursing the Major and thinking how unlucky they were to have him along on this of all nights. They were young, though. When you were young, you didn't much care whether available cunt was virgin or not, whether you got sloppy seconds, thirds, fourths, fifths...ad infinitum...or not. They'd all end up more than happy with him, come (pun intended!) morning. Ah, sweet youth!

Megan was petrified. Up in the attic, she hadn't really expected the Gestapo to arrive. Or, had it been intuition which had had her wiggling her ass like a whore and begging to be stuffed with Max's hard Jewish cock before it was too late? Whatever, she hadn't gotten the Jewish cock when she'd wanted it. She feared she would now get a little more than she'd bargained for, especially as regarded her first-time fuck.

Sonnenburg ran his belt through his left hand and looked down on Megan. Very attractive, this bitch! It was surprising how attractive some of them were. Oh, they certainly didn't have a pure and classical Aryan beauty. The Jew kind of beauty—if there really were such a thing—was decidedly more exotic. It bespoke cluttered bazaars, back-room money-changing, and unshaved beards and armpits. The Major could and did get excited by it. Oh, certainly not so excited that he automatically went hard upon seeing it. But then, nothing was that potent an aphrodisiac or, for that matter, had ever been.

My, how excitingly, enticingly, frightened she looked. Such big brown eyes, so wide with fear. How she trembled. There were goose bumps all over her little titties. Such firm little jugs. The Major bet they would each fit nicely in the palm of one hand. They would make nice mouthfuls, too. Their nipples were large, quarter-size. Megan's ribcage was so pronounced that he could count each and every bone. Her belly was concave between her two prominent hipbones. She could definitely use a little fleshing out. Too bad, she had so little chance of ever managing that.

"Frightened, are you, my little piglet?" he asked.

He didn't bother paying any attention to her answer. Her words came out muffled through her gag. He had used the Jew boy's discarded shorts, from the attic, to stuff her mouth. The shorts were pee stained at their crotch. They had a run of brown shit soiling their backside. Unclean pig, the horny little Jew-boy bastard! But the pee and shit left on his shorts must only be making Megan's mouthful more interesting. The ball of spit-soaked cotton was held in place by a strip of sheet ripped from the attic bedding. Strips from downstairs bedding tied

Megan's wrists to the headboard and her ankles to the footboard.

Sonnenburg always gagged his women. He liked to think himself a bit more refined than, say, Colonel Saber. He found un-muffled screams grating on his civilized ears. He compared them to fingernail scratches along a blackboard. To enjoy them bespoke a primitive side he found detrimental to his self-image and to his pleasure.

Megan was more than cold. She was freezing. Her condition wasn't just from the temperature of the room, either. In fact, it had more to do with her being tied to the bed and being at the mercy of this Gestapo Major. Not knowing what to expect was unnerving. What did he want? Her body? How could he want her body when his cock wasn't even erect? How could he ever hope to take her with that pitifully flaccid piece of tubing hanging, barely visible, between his flabby thighs?

Oh, Major Sonnenburg was definitely thinking of fucking Megan. He was also aware that his cock, in its present state, was hardly prepared for the battering down of virgin doors. However, he was making preparations to remedy that. He would do so the way he had done for years. As it had always worked before, he was confident it would work for him now.

He brought his belt down hard across Megan's belly. The leather made a whooshing sound on its swing through the air, followed by a resounding whack as it met with Megan's tender young flesh.

Megan screamed. Her sounds came out muffled through her gag. Yes, the Major definitely preferred those sounds to any raw-edged squeal or untempered wail. This way, her protests came out almost a loud purr, or as if she were merely having a good time.

He hit her again. This time, the leather landed hard across her young titties. Her small jugs jiggled beneath the force of the blow. They shook like little nipple-tipped mounds of gelatin. He hit her again and watched her belt-molested flesh flush in stripes of bright red.

Red stripes soon merged with pink stripes which merged with more red stripes. Megan's titties went scarlet all over under the Major's ravaging belt. Her nipples became sore, swollen, and battered.

His beating achieved a recognizable rhythm. Megan was able to anticipate each new contact of leather against her flesh. Her correct anticipation didn't lessen her pain. Quite to the contrary, it increased it. Each split second before the belt whacked into her pale skin, Megan automatically flexed her muscles. Her body met the whipping belt in taut shuddering impact.

Sonnenburg worked intently, methodically. He kept his eyes focused on each separate area he battered. He beat her tits and nipples bloody.

Finished momentarily with her jugs, he worked downward, over Megan's belly. An uncontrollable torque of the girl's body brought his belt down sharply on a hipbone. The resulting pain added itself to the other waves of agony coursing through her.

She cried in pain and in frustration. How had it all come to this? What pleasure could this Nazi have in beating a poor defenseless Jew?

If she wasn't sure of any answers to that, then neither, really, was Sonnenburg. He only knew that there was pleasure to be had in beating. Oh, yes, there certainly was. The evident little jerks of his penis were more than evidence enough for him.

His cock was definitely in the process of erection. Admittedly, it wasn't going hard at breakneck speed, but it was leaving behind its previously pathetic flaccid state for something a bit more solid and impressive. In a little time, it would be rock hard.

He delivered belt blow after belt blow to her vulnerable body. Her flat stomach turned pinker, then red, then scarlet.

He whacked her pussy. He brought the belt length down hard, right over her narrow and compressed crack that centered the v of her legs.

For her, the pain of the lash across her cunt was unbearable. She couldn't believe the bastard had hit her in her most private and sensitive spot. What did he want from her?

Whatever he wanted, he seemed to be getting it. His cock went harder. It hadn't yet gathered the tensile strength necessary to elevate it from its droop; but, it had thickened and lengthened measurably. Fat and pulpy cock head stretched forward and now readily peeked from the cowl of the once completely-concealing foreskin.

He whipped her cunt again. He whipped her legs. He whipped her feet. He went back to whipping her belly and her tits. He hit her neck. He belt-struck her hard on her face.

"Please, God, please," she mumbled. Her voice was lost within the spit and cotton stuffing her mouth. Her saliva was washing Max's shorts. The residue of the boy's piss and shit was dissolving to butter Megan's taste buds. She sampled the musky flavors and swallowed them. She was so caught up in her pain, though, that she wasn't even aware of the meal she was eating.

Suddenly, he stopped beating.

Megan, her eyes shut tightly, could hardly believe it. She was afraid to open her eyes, afraid he was even then poised and ready to bring the belt down again.

The Major was sweating. His forehead and shaved upper lip were glossy with perspiration. His chest and belly were shiny. He ran his left hand over his wet face, down his soaked chest (his nipples were hard), and down to his slicked stomach. He fisted his cock. He smeared his prick with his sweat and a drop of preseminal dew. He stroked his cock, and it responded by going harder against his curled fingers. Soon, very soon...

Megan finally opened her eyes. For an instant, she found it difficult to focus, but her vision soon cleared so she could see him.

He stood right by the bed. He still had his belt in his right hand. In his left hand, he held his still-stiffening penis. Was her agony exciting him? Was he actually getting off on her misery and discomfort?

Yes, indeed, he was! He was getting a great deal of enjoyment out of Megan's ordeal. There was something so indescribably delicious about her youth, about her innocence, about her so completely under his power, about her virgin cunt, about her previously writhing in agony (the latter having appeared almost orgasmic).

The sting from her beating didn't stop just because the lashing stopped. Hell, no. It lingered throughout her molested flesh. There was actually an accompanying itch that enveloped her. She wanted to scratch her tits, her belly, even her cunt. The feeling was sensuously discomforting.

The Major unhanded his dick. His penis, its head now fully unfurled of its once-snouted foreskin, jerked and remained extended when left alone. Cock glans no longer pointed directly at the floor but aimed toward a far corner of the room.

The Major went to the foot of the bed. Using his left hand, he began to untie the binding that held her right leg secured to the footboard.

Was this nightmare over for her, then? Was he going to let her go? Not likely. He was a sadistic freak. He was sick in the head. If anyone should have been tied up in this room, it was him and not Megan.

He wouldn't likely be freeing her soon. Certainly not! He liked her as helpless as she was. If he wasn't so anxious to beat her presently unavailable little butt, he would never have untied her right leg.

He took firm hold of her right ankle. He lifted upward, keeping her leg stiff at its knee. He saw the delectable round curves of her ass cheeks smashed against the bed. Such luscious little buns they were, too.

With his belt in his right hand, he delivered a hearty whack to the back of Megan's right thigh. A bit of swung leather contacted her pussy from behind.

"Aggghhh!" she screamed. Her teeth bit Max's soiled shorts. The strength of her clenched jaws vised spit from the soiled cotton. The resulting drool seeped through the saliva-saturated gag and ran her chin.

Lovely! thought the Major. *Oh, yes, how very lovely!* Sonnenburg delivered yet another series of well-placed blows to thigh, to butt, and to pussy. He excitedly watched as ravaged skin bruised more and more beneath the beating. It wouldn't be long, now.

Megan struggled helplessly to get out of range. It was a useless struggle, of course. She was going nowhere, and he knew just what he was doing.

She tried to kick out at his nuts. That would have taken care of him fast enough. She couldn't kick, though. He had a very firm grip on her ankle. He had her leg aimed toward the ceiling. She was at his mercy. There was no denying it. He had her and could do anything he damned well wanted to do with her—or to her.

She cried. What else was there for her to do? She prayed for her pain to end. What had she ever done to deserve this? What sins could a virgin teen-ager have chocked up to warrant such sadistic punishment?

Eventually, the Major stopped whipping and dropped his blood- and sweat-stained belt to the floor. Complete arousal had taken him longer than expected. He'd had to beat the tasty little bitch half senseless, but his cock was finally hard. Why, you'd hardly recognize it now, standing tall, as having once been that useless piece of flaccidly hanging meat that had, just moments before, been completely hidden by his belly.

He lowered her leg. He rubbed his hard cock against her sole.

"Feel how hard my dick is, piglet," he said and pushed himself more tightly against her.

Megan's tears so blinded her that she could hardly see. The beating had made her hot, and not just on the outside. Her guts were on fire. The inside of her pussy was awash with juices on the verge of boiling.

The Major's cock against her foot, she once again wanted to kick the fat little bastard in his nuts. He wouldn't let her, though. He held her leg firmly.

Eventually, the Major bent her leg for her. He placed his left shoulder into the crook of her knee. He crawled up on the bed and pushed her thigh up over her belly, her knee suddenly lodged against her sore right tit.

He was going to fuck her. He was ready. His cock was so hard that not even virgin doors would keep it out for long. It was time for him to show this Jew bitch just what Nazi cock was like. His dick would be nothing like the inexperienced inches jutted from that Jew boy's belly. Megan's cunt was lucky it had waited for this. This was going to be a real treat!

"Please!" she pleaded. "Let me go."

Of course, Sonnenburg didn't have a clue what the gagged girl was saying, although he could guess and cared less. Even if he had known, he wouldn't have complied with her wishes. He hadn't come through this warm-up just to stop before he got down to real business.

With an animalistic grunt of his passion, he grabbed the shaft of his cock and manually placed its head to the velvety divide of Megan's virgin cunt.

Her outer cunt lips parted beneath the pressure exerted by his pushing dick. Reflexively, her ass tucked against the onslaught and temporarily frustrated his efforts for insertion.

* * * * * * *

"BITCH!" HE ANGRILY GRUMBLED. "Don't wiggle so goddamned worm-like!"

She continued to writhe, though. Despite which, he successfully guided his fat cock back into alignment on her cunt doors. This time, he didn't waste any time getting his cock head firmly lodged between her pursed pussy lips.

"Nooooo," she moaned. She didn't want to lose her cherry this way, not on the end of this puffy, fat-bellied, sadistic SS officer's wretchedly jaded prick. She might have wanted Max's cock up her guts, but not this one. God, please, not this one!

His right hand slid under her butt. The increasing weight of his chest had her right leg pressed harder and harder into the soft flesh of her tit. He saw the fear on her face, and that fear fed his pleasure. Oh, yes, this was gong to be good. This was going to be very, very good.

He gave a heavy downward hump of his hips. Simultaneously, a cupping of his hand lifted Megan's ass free of the bed and toward him.

The head of his cock struck her hymen. Like the top of a drum, the membrane stretched tauter but wasn't prepared to break easily.

He grunted and put more pressure behind his cock. He was determined to enter where no man's cock had been before. And, if he'd ever had even the slightest doubt that hers was virgin territory, he now had no doubts at all. His cock battled her twat's last defenses before unexplored territory. Her flimsy stretch of protective skin was no match for his determined erection, or for his growing, downright desperate, sexual need.

"Noooooooo," she squealed. "Please no. Please no. Please no."

But for him, it was only yes, yes, yes...

"Yes, goddamn it, yes!" he grunted, and her hymen finally tore to let his cock race quickly through the raggedy-flapped gap. "Ohhhhh, baby, yes...yes...yes!"

She had expected pain, and it was there, all right; but, it wasn't of the intensity she expected. After the pain of the beating she'd endured, this pain was nothing. In a way, it was disappointingly anticlimactic.

His breath was hot and fast on her throat as he began to fuck her in earnest. He wasn't about to waste time. He hadn't even waited for her pussy to adjust to the unique feel of first-time hard meat pumping inside it.

He was hot. He fucked his dick in and out of her slippery hole. He became bolder and fucked harder and faster. Oh, God, but it was just as good as he knew it would be. There was nothing, but nothing, better than virgin piglet snatch—unless, of course, it was pure-Aryan pussy (virgin or otherwise).

Megan again shut her eyes and decided she must simply endure. What more could she do, after all? She was helpless. She was tied. She was fucked (in more ways than one). Cock up her pussy was nothing like she'd imagined and had hoped it would be.

There was nothing at all turn-on about this fat man huffing and puffing on top of her, stirring his cock between her legs. If she suspected it would have been different with Max's cock inside of her, she somehow knew that she'd never have access to Max's cock for comparison.

The Major was so excited, he almost kissed her. He caught himself just in time. A German didn't kiss a piglet! A German could fuck one, yes. Never, never (shudder!) kiss one. Kissing one and fucking one were two different things. He bit his lip to discourage even the impulse to kiss her, then kicked his fucking into higher gear.

Lying there, determined just to endure and nothing more, Megan somehow, finally, disassociated from the brutality of what was happening to her. She didn't know how she did it, but the pain of her beating and of her rape was definitely beginning to recede. Maybe she was merely in numbing shock.

The Major's big cock drove harder. It moved faster. Its outward pulls withdrew it to its barbed head, and its inward shoves penetrated to his balls. He rolled his hips. His prick deep-stirred her pussy.

She was perturbed when her hips began jerky little responses. Her lower body was reacting in primitive reflex, and she didn't appreciate it or her inability to control it. She didn't want this German scum misinterpreting that she was in anyway enjoying his brutish assault. She was a victim, in no way a willing participant. To enjoy this fuck, even an infinitesimal bit of it, would be as perverted as the man himself.

The Major could tell when her movements became more than just struggles of protest to his snake-like cock plowing her guts. He'd fucked enough women to know when he was getting to one of them. Yes, he was still able to get the juices roiling in the women he screwed.

Her hips rocked from side to side. At the same time, there was an almost imperceptible bounce to her lower body.

His fat belly pressed against her thin form. His hard cock kept tying to plow her more deeply. Like a rutting animal, he growled into her neck. He screwed faster, wilder, and more urgently. His balls gathered within his tightly shrinking scrotal sac.

She grunted softly into her gag. Pleasure? God, surely not pleasure!

He continued his hump. Boy, it was great! He hadn't been buried up a tight little piglet cunt like this—Aryan or otherwise—for a very long time. He'd almost forgotten how good it could be. A hot little bitch he had here, too. But then, all Jewish women were oversexed whores. All of them took very little to get them wound up and hot to trot. You could do anything to a Jewess once you had her properly primed. You could piss on her, shit on her, string her up by her nipples, and beat her to within an inch of her life. Then, you could fuck her, and she'd respond as if you were the greatest lover alive. Jewish women were wired to respond like that. It was their basic primitive instincts checking in. All Jews were prehistoric pigs from the same sty.

Megan's world was more and more compressed by the fuck, until finally it was just she and the fat body moving up and down atop her. She tried to expand her reality by again actively straining against her bonds and by reminding herself just what was happening to her.

An unwelcome sensation took root in the base of her belly and began to expand from there. Quite beyond her control, her hips moved even more noticeably now, taking on a life all of their own. Her ass quivered and bounced on the bed. Helplessly, she shifted her pelvis from side to side as new juices lubricated her ravaged twat.

She knew an upcoming orgasm when she felt one building. She'd masturbated her clit to enough climaxes to recognize all the signs. She could also tell that this one was going to be different than all the others. This explosion was building way down within once-virgin territory that her finger had never touched. She fought against it. No way did she want it or any trace of it. She didn't want this bastard to know that his jaded and sadistic penis could actually get to her in anything but a violently horrendous way.

She renewed the intensity of her struggles to be free of the bed, the man, and his cock. Her wrists went numb from the tightness of her bonds. Still, she fought to break free. The harder she struggled, though, the more she was aware of what was continuing to swell toward bursting inside her. Oh, God, why wouldn't somebody help her?

He dragged his sweaty face down one of her titties. He tucked his butt in and up under her ass. He pumped away at the girl's tight pussy with a series of rapid staccato punches. He put his mouth over the tip of one of her tits, his teeth around a taut-nub nipple.

With a bestial grunt, he rammed his cock in a finishing deep plunge and ground it securely into place. His balls let loose a blast of cum that burned the inside lining of her cunt sleeve.

His teeth went tighter on opposite sides of her nipple.

For a quick second, all Megan knew was the wash from his cum-spewing cock up her guts. Then, there were the lightning jolts of pure heat and energy that exploded inside her. Every muscle in her body went taut. Her toes splayed.

Major Sonnenburg bit the tip off her nipple and dined upon raw pork and the saltiness of accompanying blood.

CHAPTER FIVE

"WHERE'S SERLE?" Melissa asked, still weak from the cruel abortion of her baby. The past few hours had been a haze of pain, unconsciousness, appearing and disappearing faces, more pain.

She had been taken from a cot in some dark room and brought here to sit on a hard chair. *Here* was another room, brightly lit, like an operating theater. There was even a table with stirrups that Melissa recognized as the same used by doctors giving uterus examinations. The man now in the room with her, though, was *not* dressed like a doctor. Like everyone else who had emerged through the fog of her last few hours, he was dressed entirely in uniform-black.

He wore captain chevrons and the *Schutzstaffel* insignia.

"Ah, by *Serle,* you mean, your young Lieutenant," he correctly assumed.

"Where is he?" she repeated.

"Under the circumstances, it's decided that I, not he, take charge."

"What's happening?" she asked. "Has anyone called my parents?"

She tried hard to maintain some poise and control. It was very difficult. She wore a lone hospital nightgown tied only at its neck. Her back and butt were bare against the wood of her chair.

"I'm Captain Stahlhelm." He walked toward her. His hair was light brown. His eyes were blue. He had a ragged fencing scar that stretched from his right cheekbone to his jaw. The edges of the scar puckered when he talked.

He slapped her hard across the face with no warning. He did it twice more: once with the palm of his hand, once with the back.

She thought her head exploded.

"I'm the one asking the questions," he said. "The sooner you realize and accept that, the better it will be for you—and for me."

"There has been a terrible mistake." She tried hard to keep from crying.

"There has been no mistake, terrible or otherwise," he disagreed. "The powers that be don't make mistakes."

"Serle can explain," she said with a sob. But could he? Serle had hit her, too. Serle had killed their baby. Serle had called her *a Jew*. It was doubtful that Serle would satisfactorily explain anything to anyone.

The Captain hit her again. If possible, this time was even harder than the three he'd delivered beforehand. It knocked her completely out of her chair and onto a floor that was operating-room tiled, polished, sterile, and cold.

"You are to speak *only* when spoken to," he said. "Do you think something as simple as that can register on your minuscule porker brain?"

84

"I'm not a Jew," she insisted. There had been a mistake. Serle had called her a Jew. Now, this Captain called her one. She was being confused with someone else.

"You *are* a Jew," he said and kicked her in her stomach. The toe of his boot completely buried in her belly. It took her breath away, reminiscent of when Serle had punched her with a doubled fist and terminated the life of their child then growing in her womb.

"I'm *not* a Jew!" she screamed at him, again, and punctuated with loud gasps for air.

He kicked her again. This time, she rolled with the punch. After which, she scuttled across the floor on all fours as far as one wall.

He called for assistance and got it from two black-uniformed young men who appeared from seeming nowhere.

"I want this bitch secured to the table," Captain Stahlhelm instructed.

The two men had been called upon for similar assistance before. They knew just how to come at Melissa to subdue her successfully with the least possible effort. They moved skillfully, easily, like graceful panthers stalking an obviously weakened prey. One of them distracted her attention for the quick second it took for the other to grab her feet. Once having her feet, the youth pulled. Melissa's lower body folded out beneath her, her head whacking the wall. The jarring telegraphed pain through her brain. Blood remained where her head banged the plaster.

They gave her little chance to fight. They were on her like ants on sugar. They had her arms and legs held tightly. They carried her like a sack of potatoes over to the table and laid her on it.

She tried to struggle but had a very low strength reserve. What little energy she had left quickly drained as she realized her rebellion was a worthless exercise. All of her efforts gave these men less bother than a slightly pesky fly.

Using belts and straps available as part of the equipment, they secured her wrists, one to each upper corner of the table. They secured her feet in and to the stirrups. Finished, they left the room.

Captain Stahlhelm strolled leisurely to examine their handiwork.

"So, you're the porker to whom Lieutenant Schelling has been stupid enough to get himself engaged. Lucky enough for him, the mistake was found in time. Not that his marriage to a conniving Jew would ever have been upheld by legitimate German law. The loss of his half-mongrel bastard was another stroke of luck for the Lieutenant. That he delivered the aborting blow will look good in his record, too."

He knew Lieutenant Schelling. He knew the Lieutenant's uncle. He liked them both. The sooner this distasteful business with the clever Jewess was over, the better it would be for everyone. Honestly, it was simply annoying the length these animals would go to in order to get their subhuman genes upgraded by pure Aryan stock. Innately, they knew they could only civilize their offspring by diluting their Jewish blood with a human strain. Undoubtedly, from the very beginning, Melissa was part of a conspiracy to entrap Lieutenant Schelling's rich and pure German sperm for cultivation within her tainted Jewish belly.

Still, the Captain had to say that Serle certainly had a way of picking the best of the worst. This one was a decidedly attractive subhuman, as far as the subhuman species went. Like weeds that occasionally produced beautiful flowers, the Jews best-looking progeny were sicked on the prime youth of Hitler's Aryan Germany. Well, thank God, all Jews, unlike most weeds, *would* be exterminated in the end.

Yes, he could certainly see how Serle could spend some time plowing this slut's delicious pussy. It looked tight, even slightly agape as it was now. It was a snug little purse, to suck up the sperm of the master race. Well, luckily, there was no longer any chance whatsoever that any fertile pure-German seed would actually take root within it and spawn one or more inhuman creatures.

Melissa wondered what the Captain was thinking. He'd been staring non-stop at her cunt. He'd even pulled back the tenting of nightgown which had covered her legs.

Suddenly, he left her for a small metal table by one wall. He came back with a large pair of scissors.

"Let's look more closely at what Lieutenant Schelling found so fascinating, shall we?" He put the opened scissors to the cloth still spanning Melissa's legs. He cut until the edge of the lower scissor blade jabbed Melissa's hairy mons. He continued, cutting cunt hair and material.

She couldn't help shiver at the cold metal against her skin. What would happen if the scissors slipped? They could cut her badly. They could maim her. Worse, they could kill her. And after the cutting, maiming, or killing, what did it matter that it all had been a wretched mistake? To whom would the guilty parties apologize? To her? To her mutilated body? To her corpse?

If she could just reason with him, he would surely realize his mistake. He certainly would see she was no Jew. Every time *she* thought of her being mistaken for one, the very idea was so ludicrous she almost laughed out loud. It was only a matter of time before he discovered the mistake. If only she could buy herself enough time so that nothing drastic was done before she could be saved from the tragic results of some bureaucratic error in paperwork.

Yet, something made her keep her mouth shut. Maybe, it was what had happened just minutes before, when she'd tried to make him see reason. Maybe, it was the definite *something* so very sinister and scary about him, about the way he leered at her and her pussy, about the way he now methodically slit the front of her nightgown from hem to neckline.

As he continued snipping, he made sure the cut material sloughed from her body. When he clipped through the last bridge of cloth, he left her naked from craw to crotch, except for the sleeves still covering her arms.

He closed the scissors and placed the resulting compound-point to the soft flesh at the base of her chin.

"One push and your piggy head is skewered for the platter," he said. "Not, I assure you, a very pleasant way to die."

Die? Jesus, she didn't want to die. She couldn't help think that everything was going to be all right if she just survived these next few minutes. If she could live just a little while longer, she would live to see herself rescued; she was certain. She hadn't yet surrendered all hope that reason would prevail. Even now, she still believed there had been a mistake that would be rectified.

He removed the scissors from her chin. The withdrawn steel-point left an ooze of bright-red blood in its wake. Her evident breath of relief proved her a bona-fide fool. Eventually, she would remember how close she'd been to death at this moment and rue her bad luck in not having died, right then and there. What idiots they all were!

He took the scissors back where he'd gotten them. He came back to her and took hold of a crank on the side of the table. The table's top half began to rise. Melissa thought of hospital beds reconfigured for patients' meals.

Eventually, she had a good look down her naked tits, belly, and thighs. Her feet were hooked in the stirrups; her thighs were open wide with her cunt in the exact center. She couldn't see the actual slash of her pussy, but she saw the growth of black hair veed along her lower belly.

The Captain stopped cranking. He stood so Melissa saw him better.

"Some of my compatriots begin a first session by immediately asking their questions," he said, the edges of his scar puckering on his cheek as he did so. "I don't. I sometimes don't ask questions until the second or third sessions. Sometimes, I don't even ask questions at all. My subjects simply volunteer the information on their own. I'm hoping that's what you'll do. It shows so much more cooperation if you volunteer information, don't you agree?"

"What information could I possibly have of interest to you?" Melissa wanted to know.

He took her right nipple between a forefinger and thumb. He squeezed and twisted.

"Ahhhhhh!" Her pain was so great that she thought he'd torqued her nipple completely free of its tit.

"A yes, or a no, would have been sufficient reply," he said and finally released the pressure. "Certainly, it would have been preferable to any attempts by you to feign continued ignorance. Lest you still harbor any illusions that we're mistaken in all of this, we've already gotten all we need on you from Marta Solomon."

Marta Solomon? Melissa now had definite proof something was amiss. She didn't know a Marta Solomon. Solomon? Obviously a Jewish name. She knew no Jews. The only Marta she knew was Marta Steiger. Marta Steiger was pure-blood German. Could this man and his superiors somehow have confused Marta Steiger with this Solomon Jewess?

She wasn't supposed to speak until spoken to, but she couldn't help make a try at pointing out the mistake so obviously made.

"I don't know any Marta Solomon," she said and rushed so that she could get everything said in one breath. "I *do* know Marta Steiger. Obviously a mistake..."

"*Your* mistake," the Captain interrupted. He gave her a twisted bemused smile—one a facially deformed father might give a recalcitrant daughter. "We already know there's no *real* Marta *Steiger*."

She was going to protest. He anticipated. One hand to each of her breasts, he tented his fingers and squeezed and twisted both of her nipples. Whatever she had been going to say came out a guttural groan. The pain from her molested breast-buds helixed inward and exploded to fill her.

"Now, then," he said and gave one final turning of her nipples before releasing them, "let's just assume that I already know the names you know. And that's not too far off, you know? You're not our only information source, after all. What you tell us merely verifies what someone else has already told us. Why make such a fuss about giving us what we already know?"

What in the fuck was he talking about? Obviously, he thought he made sense, even if he didn't. How did she tell him that she didn't understand any of it? This was a nightmare. Maybe, she'd just wake up. Maybe, she'd just find she was still back in bed with Serle, sleeping after they'd made love. Somehow, she had to wake up and tell Serle she was pregnant with their baby. But then, she wasn't pregnant any longer, was she? The emptiness she felt in her belly was no dream.

The Captain walked to a sink in one corner. He filled a metal basin with hot water. He brought the basin and a bar of soap back, setting them on a small board he pulled from a slot in the table. He went to a cabinet by the wall. He came back with a straight razor.

* * * * * * *

HE SMILED WHEN HE SAW HER EYES go wide. Actually, it was always more amusing to watch the men when Dr. Senta Scheidt pulled out *her* razor. The Captain sometimes made it a point to watch the good Doctor's sessions just to see how Jewish men reacted to losing their balls. Dr. Scheidt was an expert at castrating Jew pigs.

"You'll later thank me for this bit of much-needed hygiene," the Captain said. "Your run-riot pubic hair is a spawning ground for bedbugs and other vermin."

He put the bar of soap to her twat hair. He rubbed it through her wiry strands. His cupped hand transferred water from the basin to make bubbly foam at her crotch.

He hand-stirred the suds. His fingertips curved down along her pussy crease. His fuck finger hooked her cunt. He rubbed his slick finger along the inside edges of her vagina. He pushed in. He pulled out. He added another finger. He two-finger fucked her twat.

Her body trembled noticeably. He smiled, and the scar on his cheek gave his face a decidedly macabre appearance. He was always amused by how Jew women were so easily aroused. Here this bitch was stripped down, confronted by a man, complete with razor, and she was still turned on by his fingers inside her. Any normal woman would have trembled with fear. Not Jewish cunt. Oh, no. They were hot to trot under each and every circumstance.

Melissa's snatch oozed a few drops of oily juice to mingle with the soap suds. She wondered how she could be excited. Was that natural? How could she enjoy any of this? She didn't even find the Captain sexually attractive. Was she feeling what she was feeling only because his black magic temporarily alleviated her ache, her pain, her torment, her memories? Was it because she welcomed the escape this ecstasy, no matter how it was achieved, no matter how fleeting, could give her?

The pressure at the entrance of her vagina increased. A new rush of juice oozed her pussy folds. His fingers spread her labia wider. He stroked back and forth again, letting her sensitive inner cunt become more familiar with his probing.

His continued massage of her swelling clitoris streamlined electricity from point of contact to the rest of her body.

Her hips responded. Although very little movement was available for her in her strapped position, she took advantage of what little she had.

He watched her while his fingers fucked her cunt. What sexual things these Jew whores were. No wonder they were such excellent screws. There was no coyness about them. They were ready all of the time, any time. Their pussies were forever hungry for cock and sperm. Their wombs were eternally eager to make babies; each new baby meant another Jew abomination. Jewish women were baby-making machines *extraordinaire*. They popped out kids faster than could be exterminated. Faster than rats. Faster than rabbits. Oh, how they wanted to survive! Oh, how important it was to Hitler's Germany and to the world that they didn't.

Her pussy swallowed up more of his slippery hand. Her inner cunt membranes closed inward.

She panted. His fingers moved faster and faster inside her. She bit her lower lip. She was about to climb the walls. It was obvious this wasn't the first time the Captain had finger-fucked a victim. He knew exactly what he was doing. He knew just how to play her clit and her cunt to get her most excited.

His fingers shoved deeper.

She was helpless on his sticking fingers. The fiery friction up her cunt increased. Her senses were bombarded from every side.

The roar of her heartbeat was all she heard. She was drowning in forbidden and tainted ecstasy.

She was no longer as aware of the horrors of her reality. Her world was now hazy at its edges. If she shut her eyes, she might even completely forget what existed just beyond. She could forget the Captain, the room, the razor, the table, the straps, and the bonds. She could forget everything but the glide of fingers back and forth inside her snatch. Her imagination could even fantasize those fingers as Serle's cock pumping her toward orgasmic explosion.

She trembled her orgasm over his massaging hand.

He knew he'd gotten her off. There was no mistaking the way her buttery cunt folds fluttered like crazy, sucked in and around, to swallow what they'd obviously mistaken for cock and baby-making sperm.

There were loud slurping sounds when he pulled his hand free. He didn't know why he even bothered. She wasn't here to enjoy herself, was she? Still, he didn't like to think that he was completely unfeeling. Hell, he was considerate enough even to masturbate his Doberman pinscher. This wasn't much different, except this animal walked on two legs instead of on four.

He returned to the sink for a towel. Placing it over his shoulder, he came back to her and the table. Using the straight razor, he began shaving her pussy.

She watched, fascinated, despite herself. He was actually shaving her cunt. He was scraping that private spot between her legs, revealing pale skin she hadn't seen since pre-puberty. The razor was cold against her skin. The drag of its metal on the outside of her cunt had a decidedly sensuous feel. She'd heard of women who regularly shaved their pussies. She'd never quite figured out why.

Stahlhelm performed his task deftly. His fingers moved with the expertise of a barber. He scraped hair away on the sharp edge of the razor. He wiped the blade and clipped hair on the towel. He went over most areas more than once, making sure they were completely free of bush or stubble.

When he was satisfied, he dropped the razor in the basin with a clang. He took the towel from his shoulder and dipped one edge of it in the water. He used the damp cloth to wipe all excess soap from Melissa's cunt. He then dried her de-haired skin with a dry section of the same towel.

Melissa found it all disturbingly erotic. Having never come completely down from the high she'd experienced on his hand, she had actually orgasmed while the razor was at work on her cunt. Ooze leaked from her pussy and slicked her cunt lips. He wiped the escaping juice away with the towel. He took the razor, the basin, the towel, and the soap back to the sink where he left them.

He had said nothing throughout the entire shaving process. She hadn't either. She'd finally had impressed upon her the fact that he wanted her to speak only when spoken to. She was willing to oblige him for the time being. However, she would find, eventually, some way to make him see just what kind of a horrible mistake he was making.

He didn't immediately return to the examination table. He went to one of the shelves hung from one wall. He located a shallow wooden box and checked its contents. He shut the box and brought it to Melissa's table.

She watched, fascinated and curious. A couple of times, she came close to asking him what he was doing. She'd had second thoughts. It was better not to provoke him again—quite yet.

"You," he said and provided her with what might be the facsimile of a smile, "are number *three hundred twenty-two*."

She didn't have a clue whether his strange and indecipherable comment warranted a reply or not. Not sure, she kept her mouth shut.

"You might think that unfortunate; but, think of poor *one thousand three hundred twenty-two*."

Obviously, he tried to tell her something in some kind of code? Three hundred twenty-two what? Was that Melissa's assigned number in this madhouse?

Again, he opened the box. She could see what was inside, but that did very little to assuage her curiosity. She couldn't identify even one of what she saw. Oh, there were small jars, but full of what? Some kind of paint? Were those needles? And, what was that thing that looked, but not quite, like the handle of an old fashioned ink-pen without its nib?

He picked up the instrument in question. He held it in one hand while he unscrewed the lid of one jar with his other. From the jar, he removed a sharp needle. He affixed the needle to the tip of the instrument. He flashed Melissa another grotesque smile.

"What are you going to do?" she asked. She couldn't help herself. She had to know.

Immediately, his smile disappeared.

"I thought you had learned to keep your Jew face shut," he said.

She wanted to say more. It was only by the greatest willpower that she didn't. It didn't take a high IQ to see that she wasn't in any kind of bargaining position. Hell, she was strapped securely and helpless. For one reason or another, he was convinced she had reason to be there. It was doubtful he'd ever be convinced otherwise. How many times a day did he hear how many people, each as guilty as sin, swear up and down that they were as innocent as a newborn? If Melissa was to be rescued, it would have to come from some other quarter than Captain Stahlhelm. She just hoped to hell that rescue came soon—and in time.

He took position inside her parenthesizing legs. He pulled up a stool and sat down. He looked like a writer with pen. His intended paper her pussy?

In apparent afterthought, he got up and went back to the sink. He returned with a fresh towel. He reclaimed his seat between her legs. He was ready to begin. Begin what?

He was going to stick her cunt with that needle! He was out of his mind!

* * * * * * *

"YOU CAN'T!" SHE TOLD HIM. If he thought she was going to say nothing, while he poked holes in her pussy, he was certifiably insane.

He paid no attention, which was more frightening than if he'd taken notice. He just proceeded to position the sharp point of the needle just above Melissa's hairless mons.

"Did you hear me?" she screamed. "What in the fuck do you...Aggghhhruungggh!"

He'd stuck the needle into her privates even while she was speaking. He shoved it in far deeper than it needed to go. He left it there and gave it a twist for good measure. Only then did he pull it free. A dot of blood came with it.

"You sadistic son-of-a-bitch!" she shouted. "You fucking crazy-ass Nazi bastard!"

He stuck the needle in again, then again. Each time she protested, he made sure to drive the needle in deeper.

Blood covered her skin so recently shorn of hair. He had the uncanny ability to work in spite of the slick. Occasionally, he toweled it before proceeding.

Her cunt felt stung by angry bees.

How could he perform this perversion on her? It was mad, mad, *mad!* That she was pure-blood German apparently didn't count for a damned thing. He kept on doing what he was doing. After a short while, he uncapped another jar and sprinkled soot-like powder over his man-made punctures. With the tip of his finger, he worked the black into her open wounds. He wiped away the excess powder and blood. Needle back in hand, he began hurting her again.

She was in rip-roaring pain and panic! Her teeth gritted. She whimpered like a whipped puppy. She tried to concentrate on something other than the horror ongoing between her legs, but she couldn't.

He was still tattooing a "3". Melissa could see that. He was giving her cunt the promised number: as if she were a piece of meat in a butcher shop, or a piece of merchandise in an apartment store, being marked for identification.

How would she ever explain this tattoo to a future lover or husband?

Pleeeeease stop this," she begged. Maybe if he stopped now, it would still be all right. Maybe her cunt hair would grow back and cover what damage he'd done. If only he'd stop now.

If only....

He answered her false hopes with more staccato jabs of the needle to the triangular mound of her shaved flesh. He sprinkled more black powder and worked it into her punctures.

The process continued for what, at least to Melissa, seemed forever. Finally, though, he completed the 3 and decided to take a break. He wiped up as much of her blood, and the black powder, as he could. He put the needle and its holder temporarily back into the box. He stood and stretched.

Through pain-blurred eyes, she examined what he'd done to her so far. Her sex mound was swollen and streaked with black and red. The damaged area tingled from its multiple stab wounds. She wanted to cry, but she was out of tears. Frustration and emotion so choked her, she couldn't have spoken if she tried.

Stahlhelm had worked while wearing his uniform. He now began unbuttoning his jacket. He slipped it off. He followed by removing his tie As soon as he'd shed his shirt (its sleeve, at its right cuff, dark with black powder and her blood), he revealed to Melissa (despite his remaining t-shirt) just some of his colorful tattoos—on his arms, from his biceps to his wrists. She'd never seen anything like it.

Noticing her noticing, he said: "And, you were screaming all holy hell, because of just a very few pin pricks." Disgust was evident in his voice and in the shake of his head.

He pulled off his T-shirt. More tattooing came into view. His stomach and his chest were covered with them. There were all sorts, arranged in an intricate collage. Butterflies shared space with reptiles, birds, and spiders.

Her fascinated gaze traveled his muscled chest, belly, and arms. She could tell, just by looking, that there were more yet to come—below the waistband of his pants. How far down did they go? She was perversely excited by the mere chance that he might actually show her.

He unbuckled his belt. He undid his trousers' fly. He dropped his pants around his legs. He sat and removed his boots, socks, and pants. His legs, from his underpants to his ankles, were a jumble of needle-and-ink produced forms and "things".

Suddenly, she was less concerned with her pain. How insignificant it seemed compared to what this man, standing before her, must have endured under pricking needles.

He stood, wearing only his shorts. He had a good body with well-defined pectorals, biceps, and triceps. He had ridged abdominals. All of it was pretty much covered with tattoos.

He turned his back to her. He slowly dropped his underpants over his butt. There was an eagle on his one buttocks cheek. There was a large tree on his other. There were filigree designs that trailed the small of his back into the crease of his ass.

Slowly, he started to turn around.

She licked her lips in anticipation. How could she be so excited? How could she have gone from one emotional extreme to the other in so short a time? Just minutes before, she had been completely turned off by her pain. Now, that same pain had metamorphosed into perverse pleasure. The tingling itch that reached the depth of her snatch, via the holes he'd punctured in her sex mound, caused juice to weep from between the lips of her snatch.

His cock was hard. It was long. It was thick. It was uncircumcised.

It was (sweet Jesus!) tattooed.

He walked to her. He walked between her thighs. His cock was where she could see it more clearly now. A tattooed green snake coiled its thick shaft. The snake head, on the large mushroom head of his dick, didn't have a forked tongue but a black swastika. The *Hakendreuz* was punctuated by his meatus. Even the pouted opening of his large piss hole had been stabbed by needle and stained Nazi black.

There was something else. He had no pubic hair. His crotch was as cleanly shaved as her pussy.

One hand wrapped the snake coils of his large penis and stoked languidly. Snake head slid her crack and teased its swastika into her vagina opening.

She couldn't prevent her pleasure in this tattooed man's partial insertion of his tattooed snake-and-swastika up her partially tattooed cunt.

Without further preliminaries, he rammed all of his erection inside her.

Her mouth opened and shut, opened and shut it, without her saying one word. His fat prick was so deeply embedded that she feared it punctured her belly. The bulk of it seemed determined to split her wide open.

His pubic bone ground painfully against her tender needle-holed mound. His ink-painted balls flopped her ass. He leaned forward. He put his hands on Melissa's nipples. He twisted and tore cruelly at them.

He smiled at her discomfort. With his cock still submerged to his balls up her cunt, he turned his attention back to the box. He took from it a jar of clear liquid. He pulled its stopper.

Barely recovered from the vicious thrusting which had filled her simultaneously with cock, snake, and swastika, Melissa didn't know what more he was planning; she did know it was nothing good. Therefore, she was surprised when he put the bottle, still uncapped, back in its box. Suddenly, though, the room smelled like a hospital.

"Slut-whore!" His attention was back on her.

If she was a slut, what did that make him? A sadistic bastard, that's what! A sick-o freak. What normal person had his whole body tattooed? What normal person tattooed a woman's cunt?

His hips pulled his cock free of Melissa's crack as far as his bulbous cock head. The entwined body of his tattooed snake emerged slick with her female juices.

His retrieved length of meat sped right back.

She gave a shuddering inhalation of breath. This time, he seemed to penetrate farther than the first time. How was that physically possible? It was as if his cock tip were stuck in the base of her throat, cutting off her air supply.

Once again, Melissa's pain converted to pleasure within seconds. What in the hell was wrong with her? How could she possibly be so near to dying, one minute, and on the verge of climax the next? It was a perversion she didn't like. It made her uncomfortable even to think about it. What kind of a woman was she to get pleasure, any pleasure, out of such utter degradation? He was treating her like an animal. What aspect of this disgusting mistake was exciting? How could his cock up her cunt make any of it feel right? It wasn't fair. It simply wasn't.

Fair or not, the pleasure was there. It swelled inside of her. With each powerful slide of his cock up her guts, more ecstasy stockpiled within her. Oh, God, she wished for more control over her body. Why was she made so helpless by this man? Would it be the same for *any* woman with *any* man—for *any* woman with *this* man?

She watched as he fucked her. The strange animals on his body took on lives all their own as his muscles moved beneath them. The butterfly flapped its wings. The boat shifted on wild waves. The grotesque death's-head rocked on his sweaty belly. The castle weaved in wizard's spell or earthquake.

He perspired. It made his tattoos more colorful.

She panted, her mind blank except for the pleasure she was suddenly determined to salvage even if she got nothing else from these obscene moments.

His rigid manhood slowed its cadence. The sweaty slap of his lower belly against her became less pronounced.

With his accompanying guttural groan, his cock became a freight train gone runaway brake-less on a steep downgrade.

"Ohhhhhhhh," she grunted. How could it be so bad but so good? How could she so hate it but so enjoy it? How? How? How?

His passions poised him on orgasmic brink. His cup was chock full and about to run over. It wouldn't be very long. This Jewish cunt was one sensational fuck.

His prick deeply inserted, his lower belly mated with her yawned pussy lips, he reached for the small un-stoppered jar in the box. He tipped its clear liquid over Melissa's pussy. The alcohol splashed her puncture wounds and flooded between her legs into the tender rawness of her shaved and cock-battered twat.

"God...God...God!" Her whole body was aflame, as if Hell, itself, had been conjured inside her.

His balls burned pleasurably/painfully from the overspill of liquid irritant. He was almost where he wanted to be. The roar of his impending orgasm originated down deep inside of him. Around his submerged and priming Grade-A German meat, her body spasmed again...again...again. Her cunt lining squeezed in massive convulsions that milked his dick closer and closer to cream-spill. Her screams were music to his ears, a verbal aphrodisiac that got him hotter.

The pleasure was so good. The pain of his burning balls was so good.

He grunted. The muscles of his calves went taut. The muscles of his thighs went tight. His ass muscles dimpled to rock hardness. His chest and belly muscles solidified beneath their tattoo designs. The cords of his neck stood out in high relief. His swelling cock threatened to burst the violated pussy that contained it.

He fed her wad after wad of his hot fertile German spunk. His creamy mess flooded her vagina, drowning everything in its path.

For SS Captain Stahlhelm, Jewess cunt number three hundred twenty-two was a real winner.

SS & M, BY WILLIAM MALTESE

CHAPTER SIX

MEGAN AND MELISSA DIDN'T immediately recognize one another (hardly unusual, under the circumstances), although they had known each other before—in the one-time normality of the outside world.

Melissa had been a friend of Megan's older sister, Marta. Marta was dead; *they* had shown Megan her mutilated body.

"You are certainly just as attractive as your sister once was," they had told Megan, in that dark little room where Marta's body sprawled, like a piece of shit on a slimy outhouse floor.

There were shadows in movement along the walls. Animal shadows? Human shadows? The former to judge by *their*: "Don't mind the other pigs in this sty."

"Look what happened to your sister, just because she thought she could protect a few fellow Jews. She didn't succeed, you know? She told us everything in the end. So will you."

Megan had believed them. She had known, even then, of what monstrousness they were capable. She'd been raped by the Major, hadn't she? He'd turned her over to his soldiers, hadn't he? She'd been fucked so many times, over these last few days (or, was it weeks?), she'd lost count.

She had told them all they wanted to know. She had named the names. She had revealed to them the secret of the Goermans who were really the Levis, the Natzweilers who were really the Cohens, the Rossenbachs who were really the Bersteins. They were very pleased with her responses. Hers checked out perfectly with those Marta had given them before her. See; how much easier it was when a Jew showed just a little bit of cooperation?

Back in her cell, three SS jailers took turns raping her throughout the long night.

That she eventually ended up in the same cell as Melissa was a mistake in paperwork (no matter that everyone involved would have denied responsibility). According to procedure, prisoners who knew each other, or had known each other, were never brought together after arrest. In fact, great caution was supposedly taken to keep them apart. Keep wives away from husbands, fathers away from sons, mothers away from daughters, brothers away from sisters, friends away from friends, and the sub-humans had been observed to lose heart faster. Isolate them from friends and associates, and with whom could they conspire? Such isolation, too, made it easier to tell them a mother had died, a father had been castrated, a brother had been disemboweled, a friend had named names; who was there to say otherwise?

However, the SS and the Gestapo (a part of the former), had the same problems as any bureaucracy. Tons of paperwork passed over desks and through offices every day. Mistakes *were* made. What with the sheer volume of dissidents rounded up and being rounded up, it was impossible to know what Jew knew what Jew, where and when. *Geheime Staatspolizei* bureaucrats tried their best, but they *did* lose track.

Even if they had known, in this particular instance, it would possibly have made little difference. The cell was for transient prisoners put there only until paperwork could put them elsewhere.

Megan was headed for Ravensbrook. Melissa was headed to oblivion.

Under normal conditions, it might have been too short a time for the two women to grow close. However, these were not normal times and not normal circumstances.

Any prisoner, especially women, had certain things in common, shared horrors that made them potential soul mates—even if they'd never met before.

Melissa spoke first. She had so often said what she had to say to apparently deaf ears, she welcomed a possibly sympathetic ear. Maybe her cellmate would, somewhere, somehow, get out word of Melissa's arrest where Melissa had been unable to do so. Even then, Melissa retained hope of rescue.

At first, Megan didn't believe the wretched woman, tossed like garbage into the darkness with her, was who Melissa said she was. Megan thought it some kind of trick being played on her by her captors. In that, the Melissa Goerman who Megan remembered *had* been beautiful. She *had* been young. She *had* been full of life. But then, youth, beauty, and life *could* fade easily in a place like this.

Megan began to cry, because—whether or not this woman was who she said she was—Megan had provided the Gestapo with the Goerman's name. She had told that they were Jews masquerading as pure-blood Germans. She had likely put Melissa, whether this one, or the real one, through hell by trying to save herself—uselessly, as it turned out—from the same.

She was consoled by remembering, though, that Melissa had been arrested before Megan met the same fate. Reputedly, Melissa had been snapped out of bed, which she'd shared with her German lover, only a couple of days after Marta's arrest. Was it the confession of Megan's sister, then, which had betrayed Melissa? Megan tried to remember the names already on the Gestapo list shown her after her own confession, by way proving to her they'd known what she'd known all along. Had the Goermans been listed? It was so hard to remember much of anything anymore.

"The Gestapo has somehow mistaken me for a Jew!" Melissa could still shake her aching head at the ridiculousness.

"You mean, your parents never told you?" If this were the real Melissa, Megan hardly found such ignorance possible.

"Told me what?" Melissa was confused. She'd been hurrying through her story. She wanted to get it all out. She wanted someone else to know it. Then, they could tell it to someone else who could tell it to someone else. Somewhere, sometime, it would get out that Melissa Goerman had falsely been arrested. It would get out that there'd been a horrible mistake. So, why wouldn't her cellmate let her finish? Why the interruption? There might actually be so little time left.

"If you're really Melissa Goerman, then your father was Fritz Goerman, yes?"

"You knew my father?" What in God's name did Melissa's father have to do with this, except that, maybe, he could pull some strings and get her out of this mess—if he could somehow just be told what had become of her? But how was he ever going to find out when so few people knew what had happened?

"I'm Megan *Steiger,* Melissa," Megan said.

"Megan Steiger?" Where *had* Melissa heard that name before? Not Megan. *Marta.* Marta Steiger. Megan had told the Gestapo captain they'd made a mistake, that she knew Marta Steiger not Marta *Solomon.* How long ago was that captain? God, but it seemed years. He'd told her there was no Marta Steiger. Melissa had come to believe him. To prove him a liar, though—could it really be?—here was Marta's baby sister.

"My God!" Melissa said, a piece of her sanity restored. "Don't tell me they've mistaken you for a Jew, too. And Marta?"

"Marta is dead," Megan said. Again, the vision came to her of her sister's rotting corpse, one eye and one ear missing, jagged scars on tits, on belly, on love mound. Megan shuddered.

"Dead?" Melissa didn't understand. So, maybe the captain hadn't lied to her. Maybe he'd meant Marta was *dead* when he'd said, "There is *no* Marta Steiger."

"The Gestapo killed her," Megan said. Because they'd killed her sister, Megan had named names.

The Gestapo had been very pleased. And they'd put her in a cell. And they'd raped her, raped her, raped her.

"Why would the Gestapo kill your sister?" Melissa was confused—not unusual these days.

"Why do they kill *any* Jew?" Megan shrugged.

"Any *Jew*?" Melissa's eyes narrowed. This was definitely some kind of trap. Once again, they were trying to fuck with her mind. She scuttled into deeper shadow, convinced there was no way this could be Megan Steiger, Marta dead, Marta *and* Megan *and* Melissa all victims of mistaken identity.

"Melissa?" Megan slowly scanned the darkness for her. She heard her move, but she could no longer see her.

Melissa closed her eyes and tried to come up with a picture of a remembered Megan Steiger.

Black hair. Black eyes. Thick eyelashes.

Melissa opened her eyes. The vision so clear behind her closed lids was strikingly similar to the face (this one filthy) once again close to hers in the darkness.

"Melissa?" Megan reached out a hand and ran her fingers gently along Melissa's battered cheek, down her neck.

"Oh, Megan," Melissa whispered. More horror of her circumstances dawned on her. "Marta was a Jew?"

"We are all Jews, aren't we," Megan answered simply, and it wasn't a question. "I thought you knew. While it was never anything any of us talked about among ourselves, even in private, I was sure you knew."

"I didn't know!" Melissa screamed, and her voice caught in her throat. "I still don't know." She simply could *not* be a Jew. If she were, what rescue could she ever hope to have? If she were a Jew, there would be *no* salvation. Not, anyway, in this lifetime.

"My family, your family, the Natzweilers, the Rossbachs," Megan said, "all played at masquerades."

The Natzweilers, the Rossbachs, the Steigers, the Goermans—all Jewish? That *would* explain the close clique those families had formed. That *would* explain why it had always been assumed Melissa would one day marry Heinz Natzweiler before she had frankly refused to do just that in a storm of family arguments that had lasted for months. That *would* explain why her father and mother exchanged such worried glances whenever Megan spoke of Serle Schelling. That *would* explain a thousand and one little things which had needed explaining at the time. Except it *was* too horrifically fantastic to believe!

"At first they did it for the business advantages," Megan said. "Our fathers could make money easier and faster if they weren't stigmatized by the *Jewish* label. Then, later, they stayed on to help other Jews trying to survive Hitler's Germany without false names and papers. And, you knew none of this?"

"None of it," Melissa confirmed. Oh, God, she was tired. She was so tired. She could feel her life seeping out of her like piss onto the floor.

"Dear God," Megan consoled, her voice cracking.

She reached for Melissa and pulled the woman against her. She rocked her gently, like a mother with a newborn child.

Megan's mind flashed various horrendous scenarios of Melissa and the Gestapo. She shivered. She felt physically ill. How many times had some Gestapo captain, some SS colonel, asked Melissa to reveal names she hadn't even known? How often had they not believed her and put her through even more mind-numbing tortures?

The two women stayed as they were for close to an hour. Megan just kept rocking Melissa gently. Then, by some unspoken secret mutual consent, they made love.

Or, rather, Melissa made love to Megan. Megan would gladly have reciprocated, was actually dying to lick Melissa's cunt—although, she had never licked cunt before in her life—but Melissa stopped her.

"But I want to do it," Megan protested.

"They've left me nothing *down there*," Melissa told her.

They left it at that. Some things that were better left unsaid.

Melissa pushed Megan back onto the hard concrete floor. She firmly pried Megan's knees apart. She worked herself into Megan's opened legs. She pushed up Megan's skirt and put her face in close to the girl's cunt. Megan wore no underpants; they hadn't allowed her to keep hers; they'd joked about it when she'd asked them for their return, telling her wearing any would only get in *their* way.

Melissa looked at Megan's cunt. She bent her head into it and kissed its lips.

"Ohhhhhh," Megan sighed. She'd never had her pussy eaten before—by a man or by a woman. She was a little embarrassed to be having it done now. Except that Melissa had wanted to do it; and, it somehow seemed so right at the moment. It was the first time in ages that anyone had wanted to do something to pleasure Megan. Melissa was not down between Megan's legs trying to get her own orgasm. She'd almost as much as told Megan she was incapable of orgasm any longer. She was there because she wanted to be close to someone she knew, as close as she could possibly get. She wanted to share a moment she had almost believed she was beyond sharing.

Melissa spread her tongue over that part of Megan's cunt that shielded the little clitty. She wedged herself even deeper into the gap of Megan's thighs, unaware of the strong body odor because it smelled so much like her own. The cunt lips were slightly pouted. Beyond them was a thin slice of glossy pink. Melissa's tongue tasted the latter, and it was good.

If this was the first time Megan had her pussy eaten, it wasn't a first for Melissa who had gotten in a lot of practice going down on Dr. Senta Scheidt. Dr. Scheidt liked to have her cunt licked. She liked a lot of other—genuinely perverse—things, too. She'd been fond of Melissa—for awhile. She'd actually been kind to Melissa—for awhile. However, with all of the Jewish fish presently to be found in Dr. Scheidt's pond, of which she had her pick, it was inevitable that she would eventually tire of Melissa. In the end, she hadn't been kind at all.

She'd been downright crueler than any of the men had ever been.

This, though, was the first cunt Melissa had ever *wanted* to eat. She wanted to eat it, because she needed so desperately to love somebody. She needed to be close to someone. And, Megan was from the old life. Megan was from *before the terror.* Melissa would have liked to return to that other life. This shared moment, she felt, was going to be as close to that other life as she was ever going to get.

She parted the cunt lips with her fingers. She licked the revealed clitoris. The point of her tongue played with the small button while the clitty grew firmer beneath her oral teasing.

Melissa eased Megan's left leg up until its knee touched the younger woman's stomach. She pushed her other leg up. She filleted Megan's thighs on the concrete floor. The movement made Megan's pussy lips stretch even wider. Her slick inner lips pouted and came more unstuck along their buttery seam.

Megan held her knees open, watching Melissa at work at her cunt. Simultaneously, she felt the pleasure from Melissa's eating. It was so exciting to have Melissa's tongue licking at Megan's sensitive private spots.

Melissa's tongue moved back and forth along the cunt flesh. It rolled and stuck deep to taste the warm oils basting Megan's pussy membranes.

Megan had never felt anything quite like it. In response, her buttocks began small rocking motions. The movement was very slight, but it indicated Megan's growing state of excitement. Juices were genuinely starting to boil inside of her twat and for

Melissa they had an exotic flavor and a musky perfume-like smell.

Melissa fastened her mouth tighter around Megan's vulva. Megan's young body went rigid. She bucked helplessly under Melissa's feeding and caressing mouth. Her clit went even more rigid as Melissa's hot tongue continued to lap at it.

Megan whimpered, her sounds child-like.

"Ohhhhh," she cooed.

Melissa worked her hands underneath Megan's humping little butt. She could feel Megan's cunt membranes shifting and pulsing and leaking beneath Melissa's slurping lips.

Megan quivered. Her body went stiff. And when, in the past, would she have ever imagined any of this? A few short days ago, she'd still had her cherry, and now she had been fucked and fucked, and was being eaten out by one of her sister's old friends. She *had* been Megan Steiger. Now, she was Megan Solomon, Jew, about ready to climax on Melissa Levi's eager tongue.

Melissa smacked her lips against the pussy. It shivered the length of Megan's tensed body.

The walls of Megan's cunt clenched in around Melissa's stabbing tongue. Every muscle in Megan's body contracted right along with it. Megan rocked violently in the waves that came to take her. She gasped. She threw back her head. She groaned.

Swell after swell of pleasure swept through her and swept her momentarily out of her cell and into a world that was still the way she remembered it.

Her ecstasy billowed higher, peaked, began to recede.

Melissa came up for air. She went into Megan's awaiting outstretched arms. They kissed, sucking hungrily on each other's lips and tongues.

"Was it good for you?" Melissa asked finally.

"God, yes," Megan sighed. "I wish I could find the words to tell you how good."

"You already have." Melissa pulled her closer.

They rested, each lost in thought.

"I told them, you know?" Megan broke the silence. "They showed me Marta's corpse, or what was left of it; and, I told them everything."

What was she looking for? Absolution? Did she really want Melissa's forgiveness for something she couldn't forgive herself?

"It's okay," Melissa graciously conceded. If anyone knew of what the Nazis were capable, Melissa knew. Whether it was really okay or not, the real judgment call would come from a higher authority than she.

"I told them everything I'd learned from my father," Megan said. Melissa's forgiveness had seemed to come too quickly. Did Melissa fully realize the extent of what Megan had done? "I told them about your family."

"And what did Marta tell them before you?" Melissa asked. "Do you think they actually let her die without talking? Do you think that if she knew my family's secret she took it with her to the grave? And when she did tell them, do you think she really wanted to? They have a way of making you do things, say things, you wouldn't normally even think of saying or doing."

"Yes," Megan agreed. Maybe Melissa *did* understand and forgive her.

118

"Do you know what I regret?" Melissa asked after a short while. Then, since the question was purely rhetorical, she went on to answer it without waiting. "I regret that I didn't have the names to give them. I wanted so badly to give them names that I found myself more than once making names up. Maybe my father was smart, after all, in not telling me anything. Maybe he knew I'd blab the first time I was threatened."

They had no watches to tell them how many ensuing hours they had together. They lived only for the minute, each second as precious as a diamond had been in their one-time other existence.

When the men finally came, it was just seconds after Megan had, once again, orgasmed on Melissa's exploring tongue. Their arrival was accompanied by such noise that the women were able to unclench and adjust Megan's skirt beforehand.

They arrived in their black uniforms, their black boots, their lightning-bolt and death's-head insignias. They came with their bright lights that exploded painfully on the women's dilated pupils.

The women huddled against the wall of the cell, as if pressing hard against it would disappear them into it.

"That one!" the SS captain pointed at Melissa.

Two men grabbed her, one at each arm. They pulled her away from Megan and the wall. Another black uniform entered.

If Melissa recognized Serle, she said nothing. What was there to say? She was a Jew, after all. He'd been right, all along.

He unsnapped the leather flap on his holster. He pulled the large black Luger free of its containing leather. He aimed the gun to a spot right between Melissa's eyes.

Megan watched, fascinated, afraid. She wanted to help her friend and lover, but she couldn't move. She cowered, having known, all along, that someone would come eventually to spoil whatever contentment she and Melissa had been able to scrounge from their dire situation.

SS Lieutenant Serle Schelling pulled the trigger. He did it without the least qualm or hesitation. If he had ever had feelings for Melissa Goerman, pureblood German, he had none for Melissa Levi, polluted Jew. Killing this ugly and mutilated cretin, merely removed an embarrassment from his life and blight from his career. It was better this way in that he knew for sure she was dead. He knew she wouldn't be turning up later. By the deteriorated look of her, he had done her a favor anyway.

The impact of his bullet blew off the back of Melissa's head. Pieces of her scalp, brain, cranium, hair, and blood, splattered Megan's face and body.

Megan screamed amid the downpour of human pieces. Later, after they'd left her along with the decaying corpse for three full days and nights, the young woman was forced to drag the body of her friend and lover out of their cell, up two flights of stairs. They made her lift Melissa's body into the back of a truck.

The truck was stuffed with bodies, Melissa just one more for the heap.

CHAPTER SEVEN

HE WAS BLOND BUT not *the* blond man. Anyway, she was pretty sure he wasn't. How long ago had it been since she'd seen *him*? She'd lost track of the days. Or, was it weeks? Or, was it months? Could it even be years?

She feared she wouldn't recognize him when she saw him. Could that ever possibly happen? She'd only seen him for that brief moment. There'd been all those bright lights. There'd been the horror of Melissa's exploding head.

No, she *would* recognize him. Something intuitively would tell her. God, it simply had to!

This blond man *wasn't* a lieutenant. His age was wrong, too. The blond who killed Melissa was younger—and far better looking.

Lieutenant Colonel Speidel turned to Dr. Scheidt.

"My dear Senta," he said. "You've bypassed protocols again, haven't you?"

"Colonel, whatever do you mean?"

He had an eye for the best of the female meat, and Dr. Scheidt had been chagrined to recognize that the first day she'd arrived after being reassigned to his concentration camp.

She shouldn't have believed, even for a minute, that he wouldn't find out she'd detoured Megan to the laboratory, but the temptation to do so had been too great to resist. If SS studs had difficulty finding adequate fucks, Senta's passions were no less frustrated. While she thoroughly enjoyed the sexual charge received from castrating Jewish men, her real needs lie in other directions. She hadn't had her cunt really worked over by the likes of this little Jewish bitch in a long time.

Speidel couldn't blame Senta's self-serving efforts, and she might have gotten away with them, once again, if Lieutenant Strohrer hadn't been down at the boxcars when the latest shipment arrived. "I'm afraid this young lady must be put to more useful service to the *Reich* than becoming just another of your lab rats."

Foiled, Senta figured she might as well appear a good loser. "It might prove interesting for you to at least let me complete this intended session before taking her away."

"It's not merely *me* I have to think about, Doctor," Speidel reminded with a chastising frown. "As *the* man in charge around here, I have a certain responsibility to the men under me. How do you think they'd feel if I let a seldom-seen-here decent piece of ass be ruined before they had their chances at it?"

"Ruined?" Senta summoned her very best look of innocence which wouldn't have fooled anyone, certainly not Speidel. Probably because, Senta hadn't been even vaguely innocent for a very, very long time.

"Let's just say I've seen some of the women who enter your lab, Doctor. While I was able to recognize them as female when they stepped through your front door, I've occasionally not been all that sure by the time they were carried out the back."

"Really?" Senta shook her head, as if she didn't have a clue.

"How about I personally go with you to pick a suitable replacement?" As if there was likely another such prime piece of ass that he would waste on Senta.

"But, sir," Senta said and turned on all of her charm, "what I have planned will in no way damage the merchandise for you or your men. If you'd just let me use her for the next few minutes, you can stand by and make sure I'm telling the truth. You might even lend a helping hand, or—" She gave a salacious wink. "—something *other* than a hand."

"Well," Speidel wavered. Senta had come up with some genuinely innovative entertainments in her time. There was no need to get on her bad side (she *did* have friends in high places), especially since she seemed so gracious in defeat. "I'm deadly serious that nothing should be done to make the merchandise unusable."

"You have my word." She regretted the girl so obviously heard them. It wouldn't be quite as much fun with the little bitch knowing she wouldn't be hurt. But then, she would be plenty hurt, later. Every prisoner, even this one, sooner or later became fodder for the Doctor's experiments or a fiery furnace.

A door opened, and two lab assistants entered with a young man dragged between them. The youth was completely naked, his body crisscrossed with

an intricate latticing of bloody welts. He was blond,
but it was unlikely he was the pure-blood German
he might have seemed under other circumstances.
His face was puffy and swollen. One eye was completely closed. There was a trickle of blood running
the corner of his mouth.

"Ah, our star performer has arrived," Senta said
with genuine anticipation and delight. "Strap him to
the table."

Megan watched. Did the kid look familiar? Was
Megan just thinking he did because of his blond
hair? How many blond-headed boys and men had
Megan checked out since that nightmare with
Melissa in their cell?

The youth was laid on his back and pulled so
that his knees folded over the bottom of the table.
His ankles were attached to manacles affixed to the
table legs. His thighs were secured by straps just
above his knees. A leather strap was wrapped and
secured across his stomach, another over his chest,
another over his neck. His arms were positioned
parallel to his body and manacled into place.

Speidel moved closer. He didn't know what
Senta planned, but he suspected it would, as promised, be interesting. She had a fantastic knack for
clever amusements. Such diversions were especially
welcome amid the could-quickly-get-so-boring routine of constantly stuffing Jews into furnaces.

"Bring the girl here," Senta instructed and
moved to a spot nearer the bottom of the table.

"Do take off your filthy shift," she told Megan
and watched, with great interest, as Megan did as
instructed. Megan had for so long been doing every-

thing she was told, her compliance to all orders was automatic.

Senta was delighted with what she saw stripped and naked before her. The girl was an excellent specimen, everything considered.

Her hair was in ragged tufts that stood out in all directions; someone had apparently been turned loose on it, and quite recently, with a pair of rusty sheep shears. Someone had sliced or bitten off the tip of one nipple. There was a nasty series of circular scars on her belly where someone had used her for an ashtray. There were more of the same on her cunt, but her pussy seemed, at least at first glance, perfectly viable.

At one time or another, she had been forced to take something up her ass that was just too big. However, the resulting anal rip had been sewed up by an expert and had healed so that it would have gone initially undetected by anyone but a doctor. Someone had obviously liked her butt so well that they'd gone to a helluva lot of trouble to see it healed properly (for repeats?). Senta would have liked seeing the cock, if it had been a cock, which had done the damage.

Speidel's cock, on the other hand, was definitely not any such monster.

"Now, *do* pay attention, Jew bitch." Senta said. "I'm not fond of repeating myself. So, do what I say, just as I say it, when I say it, and there will be no problems. Don't, and I'm sure even the Lieutenant Colonel will agree you'll deserve severe reprimand."

Megan had no intention of disobeying. She would live through this ordeal, just as she'd lived through all of the others. She was determined to survive until she found a certain blond lieutenant and killed his sorry ass. She'd promised herself that. She'd promised Melissa's memory that. More and more often, lately, Megan wondered if her desire for revenge was the only thing that kept her going.

She stood calmly while wire tips were adhesived to her forehead, neck, torso, arms, and legs, by the Doctor. A metal belt, with a metal plug, was attached to her midsection, the projection generously greased and snugly fitted up her vagina. Wires protruded from the belt. All wires had one end attached to a large square machine.

"Doctor?" Speidel said from his observation point. "I hope you *do* remember that the girl is scheduled to survive this exercise."

"Afraid I'm going to fry her, right before your eyes?" Had there been no repercussions, Senta might have done just that.

"I just remember the last prisoner I saw hooked to those very same wires."

"We're quite capable of *regulating* current," Senta reminded. "Rest assured that your little plaything will come through this still a suitable plaything."

Speidel adjusted the alignment of his stiffened cock along his left thigh. He folded his arms across his chest.

Megan was stood close to the boy's knees and was bent forward over the table so that her face was positioned directly over his large and flaccid penis. Her arms were extended, her wrists clamped beside his.

126

A leather harness was secured on and over her head. One of its two remaining unsecured straps, like long braids, hung down each of her cheeks. Its leather guard snugly fit her chin.

A leather strip with a buckle at both ends was threaded beneath the boy's ass. One strap of Megan's harness was affixed to one buckle, the other strap to the other. When both straps were pulled through the buckles, Megan's face was forced nearer the boy's groin.

The kid's cock was circumcised. It was a large phallic python impressively drooped all of the way to the table top between his legs. Its head was heart-shaped and deep pink. It capped a bulky cock neck that was lightly veined, except for one major run of blue that wiggled its left side from circumcision scar to cock roots. The hair at the base of his cock was blond and matched the hair on his large balls and head.

"Now, Jew bitch, take his cock *and* his balls in your mouth," Dr. Scheidt instructed. "Granted, it'll be quite a mouthful, but I'm sure you can do it if you focus your entire piggy concentration to the task."

"I don't expect her to choke to death, either," Speidel warned.

"Granted, the boy is well hung but hardly like a giant," Senta pooh-poohed. "Surely, this isn't the first cock this young lady has been requested to eat."

Megan pursed her lips. She sucked his cock head into her mouth with a resounding wet smack. Close up, she could see his cock neck had small parallel runs of scar tissue along its entire length.

The striations were bumpy against her lips. Immediately, his cock began to harden.

"Take your time," Senta directed.

His cock head reached the opening of Megan's throat. More cock thickening was evident as she sucked it deeper. She was confident she'd manage his dick, hard or soft. Taking on the nuts, too, though, was another matter.

Doctor Scheidt provided an assist by lifting the kid's scrotum as soon as Megan's lips were sucked close enough. The flaccid skin of his sac slid between Megan's lips, followed shortly by—plop, plop—both his balls.

It was certainly a mouthful, but Megan wasn't gagging yet; although, if the cock got any harder any faster....

Her nose burrowed funky blond pubic hair. Her nose had smelled far worse. Her chin rested on the hard table top. Her lips were flush with the boy's lower belly.

The straps of Megan's head harness were pulled tighter and permanently anchored Megan's face where it was over her mouthful of hardening cock and cum-swelling balls. She found it difficult to breathe but not impossible.

"Now, Lieutenant Colonel," Senta said, satisfied with progress, "about that helping hand—or *whatever*—you thought you might volunteer by way of assistance."

I'm rather hoping it's the *whatever* in which you're interested," he said. His hand was at his crotch and outlining the evident stiff ridge of his swollen meat as secured by his pants leg.

"What do you think your *whatever* could do with the likes of this?" Senta ran her hand down the smooth contours of Megan's presented-perfectly-for-servicing ass.

Speidel deftly undid his trouser fly. He reached in and pulled out just what Senta Scheidt so covetously wished she had sprouted from her own belly. He cascaded his equally desirous balls to join it.

His cock was smaller than Senta's smallest dildo, and it was certainly dwarfed by the boy-on-the-table's animal prick. It was deep brown, almost chocolate. It had a funny little bend near its head. It bulky foreskin gave it a decidedly thick look. Its meatus wasn't a mere slit but a large gaping hole. Still, a cock was a cock was a cock—any cock more cock than Senta could boast. No need bemoaning spilt milk (whether from a cow or from the Colonel's stiff pecker).

Speidel took up position behind Megan tastily inviting butt. Holding his erection in his right hand, he rubbed his cock's head along the girl's ass crease. His dick leaked moisture which trailed her buttocks.

He put his free hand to one of Megan's hips for support. His cock's tip drilled between her pliant ass cheeks and located the rubbery opening of her re-paired asshole.

Like a tapered section of rubber tubing, his cock slid into Megan's anus. Her sphincter rolled more widely open, like a camera lens, as his cock pushed deeper. Her tight anal ring pushed the Colonel's foreskin back along his entering shaft to make a thick turtleneck.

She concentrated on relaxing the muscles up her ass. She had learned through painful trial and error that there was actually a technique in taking cock up her butt. It would take a far bigger whanger than this one to give her any real problems.

Inside of her mouth, the kid's cock kept hardening.

The end of Speidel's cock lubricated its own way with pre-cum. His dick steadily slid asshole until his balls whacked up and under Megan's shapely buns. The slapping of his scrotum to Jew-bitch bottom caused the delicious ache that sunburst his groin.

He now had both hands on Megan's hips. He held tightly while a backward shift of his hips pulled his cock out to its mushroom head. The drag of his penis sucked at Megan's bowel and puckered some of it out of her asshole.

A quick buck sent his penis once more into the breach. The bulky folds of his foreskin once more sensuously slid his hard inner cock core.

His hands moved along Megan's body and down to palm her tits. Her one perfect nipple and the damaged one pressed his hands. His fingers kneaded. His hips rolled in accompaniment, stirring his cock within the little bitch's tight anal sleeve.

Senta watched, jealous as hell. God, she wished she had a real cock to put up this girl's asshole. How she wanted to experience the very same pleasure so evident on Speidel's smug gone-sweaty ugly face.

The cock in Megan's mouth was almost completely stiff. Megan couldn't help wonder if this poor kid really wanted his dick so solid. Wouldn't he, more likely, prefer no sense of excitement? Wasn't his cock betraying him as Megan's body so often betrayed her? Did he find pleasure up her mouth just as she derived pleasure in having it up there, and in having Nazi cock up her ass, and in having the metal plug secured up her pussy? What was there about the body, male or female, which made it respond sexually, automatically, even at horrible times like this? What primitive drives were there to give a boy pleasure while tied to a table, to give a girl pleasure while ass-raped by hot cock and pussy-raped by cold metal?

The round, firm hills of Megan's butt smeared the man's trouser crotch with wet sweat and mashed his balls against his pants fly.

There was very little Megan could do for the cock up her face, except vibrate her throat muscles and lave it with her tongue. To give it really memorable head, she needed more leeway. She was so harness-anchored over his dick to his balls that she couldn't pull up around it. She couldn't orally masturbate it like she would like.

So, she did what she could. She sucked. She rolled his balls against his cock. She bathed his prick with wet-warm spit. Her excess saliva drooled her oval lips and provided bubbly foam for the tabletop.

Speidel continued thrusting and pulling. Forward, back. In, out. His strokes gradually increased in speed. The friction made her fucked bowel hotter around his plugging shaft.

The cock up Megan's butt wasn't her only pleasure-giver. The metal that slotted her cunt spawned ecstasy all its own. The metal grew warmer within the leakage of Megan's hot love juice. It rubbed pleasantly against all sides of Megan's snatch.

Speidel fucked her ass with powerful, even stokes. Her undulating hips were now perfectly coordinated to match his rhythmic thrusts. Up Megan's butt, his penis ballooned larger. His moan was animalistic. He humped faster.

"I'm going to mine some Jew shit!" he grunted. "Then, I'm going...to soak...it...with good... German...German...German...cream!"

He pushed in deep. He hunched more noticeably. His lower belly ground against her naked ass. His hands held tightly to her tits. His muscles tensed.

"Jew shit...Jew shit...Jew shit...is browning my...pure-blood...white German dick!"

Dr. Scheidt pulled the switch on the square machine into which all of Megan's wires were fed.

For Megan, it was like being hit by a ton of bricks. Her hands clenched into fists. Her toes curled. Her leg and arm tendons stood out in high relief. Her ass went rock hard and dimpled around her madly collapsing asshole. Her jaws clamped.

"Aagghhhhrrrr!" Speidel growled. His cock was in full eruption. Even as it exploded, it was vised even harder by her imploding asshole. Electricity sped through his blasting dick. His balls received a residual jolt.

Senta hoisted her dress and jabbed her fingers deep up her juicy cunt. Her oozing love juice flooded onto and over her hand.

She shifted the lever of the voltage regulator, releasing bursts of lower, then higher, and then lower current.

Megan's ass hole squeezed, relaxed, squeezed. Her fists clenched, unclenched, clenched. Her vagina contracted, relaxed, contracted. Her toes curled, uncurled, curled. Her jaws clamped, relaxed, clamped.

Speidel held on for dear life. He didn't know what was happening. His body was alive with the electric jolts fed to it by Megan's wired body. His cock seemed on the verge of shooting his cum forever and ever.

Megan tasted salt. Its warmth gushed to overrun her chin, her mouth, and her nose, even while her body was jarred and was jarred again, by constant bursts of fluctuating electricity.

Above the drone of the machine and the crackling of electricity...above the grunts of Megan and Speidel, and the Doctor...another sound took precedence. It was high-pitched and inhuman.

Megan couldn't breath, still gagged by cock, balls, and blood. Desperately she tried to come up for air, but she couldn't.

Dr. Scheidt finished getting off on her hand. She pulled her soaked fingers from her pussy. Her skirt dropped. Quickly she returned the voltage regulator to zero output.

Her assistants were ready at the table and hurriedly unbuckled Megan's head harness. They, as well as Senta, were afraid the doctor may have misjudged, distracted by too much playing with her own cunt while the voltage was on.

Speidel's cock popped free. The man stumbled backwards. His legs momentarily refused to support him, and he almost fell. He was disoriented.

Senta and her assistants forcibly pulled Megan's head free of the boy's crotch. So, why couldn't Megan yet breathe? She remedied her dire situation by puking out a mess of severed penis, testicles, and blood to splatter the youth on the table.

"What the hell?" Speidel asked everyone and no one in particular. He managed to make it back to the table on which he leaned for support. He felt whipped to frothy light-headed nothingness by some giant eggbeater.

"She'll be fine," Senta diagnosed, mistaking Speidel's concern for Megan and not for himself. "She just needs to catch her breath."

Speidel's hand slipped in slime. The table, the body on it, and the floor all around were covered in blood. Senta, her assistants, Megan, and the Lieutenant Colonel were covered in crimson splashes.

The kid spasmed helplessly on the table, the ragged hole at his groin still spouting his life in liquid form. His now-flaccid penis, complete with its teeth-serrated bloody stump and bitten-off nuts, curled within the crimson pool that overflowed the concave cupping of his belly.

CHAPTER EIGHT

THERE WAS SOMETHING MEGAN was supposed to do the minute she saw him. Kill him? Yes, that was it. She couldn't remember why. There were a lot of things she couldn't remember. She spent days at a time trying to remember who in the hell she was. She never seemed to have much success.

He was blond. He was exceptionally good looking. He had his right arm in a sling. He was an SS captain. Something was wrong there. For some reason, his being a captain wasn't quite right. He should have, maybe, been a major. Or, if not a major...Megan just didn't think she was supposed to kill a *captain*. And, where did his bum arm come from? Suddenly, she wasn't sure she was supposed to kill anyone.

She tried harder to remember. There was a reason, somewhere, for how she was feeling. It must have been clearer at one time, because she'd gone to the bother and risk of getting and concealing a murder weapon, hadn't she? It was an SS ceremonial dagger. Or, had *she* gotten it. Maybe it was someone else who got it and hid it. Had it been Anna before that poor woman was summoned to the laboratory, never to return? How long ago was that?

The black-uniformed duo, of which the blond captain was one captain, marched down the row of women, slowly. Megan was less concerned with the dark-haired one whose name she couldn't remember but whom she *could* remember had sodomized her more than once.

They stopped in front of a tall Slavic girl.

"Here you are, Serle," the dark-haired captain said to the blond one. "Her cunt is a little loose from overuse, but her asshole is still tight enough."

"Jesus, where did you get these dogs?" Serle wrinkled his nose in disgust.

"Well," Captain Stern Saarbrücken said, a little embarrassed that he, personally, still found the Slav sexually desirable, "we're not exactly in Berlin. For most of these, their next stop is the fiery furnace."

"I'd say most of these women are overdue for baking." Serle moved to the next girl in line.

"You should see what those who aren't officers end up with," Stern consoled.

Serle shuddered at the mere thought.

"Maybe you should wait and come back in a week or more," Stern suggested; he spoke from personal experience. "I guarantee, they won't look half as bad to you by then."

"In a week, I hope to be in Berlin," Serle said.

"I wouldn't hold my breath if I were you," Stern answered. "They're not known for their speed in cutting orders lately. What with the war going so well, the High Command feels it safe to let its wounded enjoy extended rest and recuperation here in the lovely countryside."

* * * * * * *

SERLE HAD NO ANSWER FOR THAT.
When the war effort went badly, everyone was hot to get every available man into the field. When the war went good, there wasn't that pressure, and things slowed down except, of course, for the high priority assigned the Jew extermination program. The High Command was anxious for the Jewish problem to be handled as expediently as possible by men competent to do so. Serle just hoped he hadn't become someone seen as more suited to manage a concentration camp than perform more derring-do on the battle field. For Christ's sake—he was a soldier, not a vermin exterminator.

He continued down the line. Stern followed.

Serle made no more comments, derogatory or otherwise. There was no need to point out that these women were the dregs. Every officer knew that sad truth already.

Serle would have preferred to be back at his billets. There was something perverse in thinking a Jew cunt could, under *any* circumstances, be a suitable receptacle for pure Aryan sperm. However, he kept that opinion to himself. Too many highly placed personnel, including his immediate superiors, got their rocks off up Jewish cunt, mouth, and ass, and wouldn't look kindly on being judged by a mere SS captain, no matter his outstanding performance and wounding on the battlefield.

"How about this one?" Serle asked, standing in front of Megan.

She didn't know when she'd seen anyone so handsome.

"Well," Stern said and pointed his right forefinger to his temple to make clockwise circular motions.

"I'm not planning to fuck her brain," Serle reminded. "If I wanted to fuck brain, I'd certainly look elsewhere than to a Jew, wouldn't I?"

"Point taken," Stern said. He'd been hoping to keep this particular bitch for himself. Cleaned up, she wasn't half bad, and Jesus what a tight little ass she still had, despite all the cock, including his, which had been forcibly pumped in and out of it. So what that she was a little loony? So what that some of the officers didn't like her because she was too machine-like? One had called her "downright zombie-like!" Hell, you could slap the shit out of her, and she'd only sob silently without even trying to fight back. The guys who got their jollies by seeing a woman put up a struggle were especially turned off by her passivity. She wasn't the first little broad, though, who'd had the entire struggle sucked right out of her.

"She'll do," Serle said.

Stern pointed the way to the small fucking cubicles. Serle headed in that direction, Megan in tow. Stern stayed where he was, having not yet decided which of the Jew butt was, this time, going to get the privilege of his giant pumping German pecker. Hell, maybe he'd just wait for Serle to finish up and slide on in for some sloppy seconds.

Meanwhile, Serle was at the curtained entrance to one small enclosure. Inside was a small cot and a chair; the latter was in case an officer decided to undress and needed somewhere for his clothes. Most men didn't bother stripping beyond taking off their jacket and dropping their pants.

* * * * * * *

"I SUPPOSE ONE OF THESE fuck-holes is no better than the other," Serle passed judgment.

Megan silently disagreed by walking past him and to another opening two cubicles down. She disappeared through its curtain.

Serle was going to order her ass on back but, maybe, each girl was assigned a specific cubicle. He hoped to shit he wasn't around long enough to get all that familiar with routine. The prospect of his being stuck here for the duration of the war made him literally shudder. Even with the consolation of his Iron Cross, First Class, for bravery in battle, and his promotion to captain, this place made him feel he would have been better off had he avoided hero-of-the-Reich status *and* the bullet to his arm.

He shrugged and followed the Jewish whore.

She was genuinely surprised to see him. Not because she was the slave that this prime specimen of the Master Race had followed, but because she'd forgotten all about him. She'd been wondering what she was doing where she was instead of in the communal area with the rest of the women. Had this handsome blond man somehow picked her to service him? She vaguely remembered thinking she was about to be chosen, yet again, by Captain Assfucker. Having a faulty memory was damned frustrating—or maybe not!

"All I want from you, whore, is a quick blow-job," Serle said, unbuckling his belt. "I'd actually prefer jacking off in my own quarters, but I'm not much good at whacking my meat with my left hand."

Megan watched him ineptly manage the unbuttoning of his fly.

Did he look familiar? Was he the man she'd been waiting for? Was that why she'd somehow ended up with him in this room? Had the time finally come? But, he was a captain. Wasn't it a *lieutenant* who had blown somebody's head off? Megan should have remembered whose head, but she couldn't. God only knew how many heads had been blown off how many Jews by how many Nazis, since her nightmare began. How could she be concerned with just one head?

He dropped his trousers and underpants around his blond-blond ass and legs. He sat down on the cot, his soft cock on full display. He leaned against the wall.

"Come on, cunt." He wanted it over and done.

She knelt between his thighs.

He could have been promoted, Megan thought as she put her mouth to the head of his cock and quickly sucked at its head. A lieutenant didn't stay a lieutenant forever but made captain eventually.

Just looking at that line-up of wretched creatures had drained Serle of any pre-existing desire. He shut his eyes and concentrated on going hard. If he got his rocks off today, maybe he'd have his arm out of its cast the next time he needed his wad blown. If so, he would stay in his quarters and beat his own pud to climax. How lucky any guy (he personally knew just one) who had the flexibility to eat his own meat and avoid Jew-tainted mouth, hand, ass, and pussy.

* * * * * * *

SHE SUCKED RIGHT DOWN to his blond balls. Had someone instructed her to suck up his balls, too? Or, had *that* ordered ball-sucking been another time and place and scrotum?

Serle tried to fantasize the last time he'd received a really good blow-job. Had he even had one since Melissa? Damn, but this was no time to think of Melissa!

Serle? Megan pondered as she sucked. *Was that what someone had called this captain?* She worked her tongue around the shaft of his cock and coaxed his meat toward hardness. She rolled his hairy blond balls against the insides of her cheeks, and collided his testicles with the shaft of his cock. *Was Serle the name of the man for whom she'd been waiting?* She must have thought so. Why else bring him to this particular room?

His thighs opened wider. He automatically, despite himself, groaned in response to the pleasurable ache of his nuts squashed within the woman's cock-and-testicle-washing mouth. With his eyes shut, he didn't—thank God!—have to look at the ugly cretin going down on him.

Her face swung back up his cock. His prick still wasn't completely hard, but it was well on its way. Hell, ugly as she was, she still might have his cock rock solid in no time.

Her taut lips glided down and up his hardening shaft. Some other time, she had done this...in a harness? Had she been a horse in some other life?

Had she really seen Serle standing in a cell, his gun aimed at someone's head? Had she seen him pull the trigger? Had she been showered with the resulting spatter of human brain, and blood, and hair?

Had she dreamed the knife under this bed, beneath this floor? Was it the knife that made her lure this captain to this room and not to one of the others?

Her lips slid his dick. His penis was so hard now that she couldn't reach its cock head and still keep his nuts swallowed. So, she released his balls to pool his spit-wet scrotum on the blanket between his open thighs.

Her mouth and tongue made love to his pulpy corona. Her taste buds savored the leakage from his cock meatus. His juices were salty. Blood was saltier.

She went down over his cock again, and its rubbery head collided with her palate and careened on by.

She reached bottom, her lips among the wiry strands of his blond pubic hair. Her nose smelled him turning sweatier.

He bounced his butt ever so lightly on the bed. He dropped his good arm so that he could put its hand on Megan's head and let her know just what he demanded from her by way of her sucking cadence.

She commenced some no-doubt-about-it serious head, her throat having easily adjusted to every last inch of his German-cock inches. On each new run of her mouth over his cock, she had a superb view of what she was eating.

Lieutenant (not *captain*) Serle "Something". Blond. Blue-eyed. *Schutzstaffel. Hakenkreuz.* German. Nazi. Melissa-killer?

* * * * * * *

AS SHE SUCKED, her fingers swept the floor beneath the cot.

Anna had hidden something in this room, beneath a floorboard. They'd hauled Anna off to the laboratory before she could retrieve whatever it was she had hidden. She never came back for it, either. No one ever came back from Dr. Senta Scheidt who had harnessed Megan's head to that boy's crotch...who had run electricity through Megan's body until Megan's jaws had spasmed and bit right through erection and scrotum. There had been blood, blood, more blood. There'd been nothing for her to breathe but blood and teeth-severed cock. Except...for that to have happened, she would have had to *come back* from the laboratory, when everyone knew such come-backs never-never happened.

Serle groaned. *The boy had screamed.* If Megan had once emasculated the boy, she could now emasculate the man. Or, could she? Without the electric pulses running rampant throughout her body, could her teeth actually sever this German's cock?

Why was she even thinking of biting off this bastard's lovely German dick? There was a better way, a surer way. There was the knife, a beautiful knife with its gold and ivory handle. How had Anna gotten it without anyone knowing, without repercussions? She would never tell, because she was dead. Megan knew that for a fact without ever having seen the body. Although, she'd definitely seen Melissa's body, and the body of the boy, and the body of her mutilated sister. Bodies, bodies, everywhere, and lots of blood to drink (not to mention bitten-off cock to eat)!

The cracks between the floor boards were full of dirt. Megan's fingernails, bitten to the quick, were unlikely tools for successfully prying up any board. All of the other times, she'd used something as a lever.

Her face bounced. Her compressed lips dragged from his cock roots to his cock head, from his cock head to his cock roots. Up and down. Up and down. Round and round...and round.

He was still propped against the wall, his eyes shut. It wouldn't be long now. His scrotum was compressing. His cock was swelling even larger. His belly was spilling its aching warmth into his chest cavity.

Megan clawed at the floor beneath the cot.

She had to get to the knife! She had to kill this man. He had killed her lover. He had blown away Melissa's head. He was blond. He was SS. He was a captain in the *Schutzstaffel*.

If there was a God in heaven, surely He would help her realize this moment of sweet revenge—for Megan, for the dead Melissa, for the boy on the table, for Megan's dead sister...

Quite beyond Serle's conscious control, he suddenly fantasized his ex-fiancée's mouth on the receiving end of his priming dick.

"Suck it, Melissa, you betraying Jewish cunt! Suck it, suck it, suck it!" he ordered, his breathing erratic.

The board beneath the cot yielded to her insistence. There was a God after all.

Leutnant/Hauptmann Serle Schelling. Luger gun. Melissa Levi, alias Melissa Goerman. Megan Solomon, alias Megan Steiger. Bright lights. Love in the shadows. Blond hair. Blue eyes. Handsome face. Exploding bullet. Exploding head. Raining brains. Pieces of black hair. Flesh. Blood.

Oh, holy, fucking, shit!" Serle grunted his ascending pleasure.

She found the dagger and closed her fingers around its beautiful ivory and gold handle.

Captain Serle Schelling, lately Lieutenant Serle Schelling, of the German *Schutzstaffel*, blew his wad of rich cream into the depths of Megan's sucking throat, screaming out the name of his murdered Jew fiancée—"Melissa!"—as he did so.

SS & M, BY WILLIAM MALTESE

CHAPTER NINE

MEGAN SAT ON THE EDGE of the cot, dragging the tip of one finger back and forth through the sweat stain left by the captain's ass.

There was undoubtedly something she should be doing instead. Oh, yes, the knife. She should make doubly sure it remained safely hidden. It was such a pretty thing, all gold and ivory and steel.

She'd check in a minute to be sure the concealing floorboard looked undisturbed, all of its surrounding cracks filled with dust. It wouldn't do for someone to discover it. God, no!

She'd almost made a horrible mistake. She'd almost killed the wrong man. They would have carted her off to the laboratory or furnace. She would have been dead, and the *real* murderer of her one-time friend and lover would be beyond Megan's revenge. Oh, it was a good thing Megan had caught herself in time and had come to her senses.

This blond German captain couldn't have killed Melissa. God, no! If he *had* killed her, then Megan would have found her man, when it was *her search for him* that compelled her to survive the horrors of each ensuing day.

What was it someone had said within her hearing in that long ago and much-dimmed past? *"They're out to kill us. They're out to kill each and every Jew. They will, too, if we don't stop them. In order to stop them, we must live."*

Megan wasn't quite yet ready to die!

www.ingramcontent.com/pod-product-compliance
Lightning Source LLC
Chambersburg PA
CBHW020651180626
46816CB00003B/1222